♡The Nature Club ♡

Read more OWL DIARIES books!

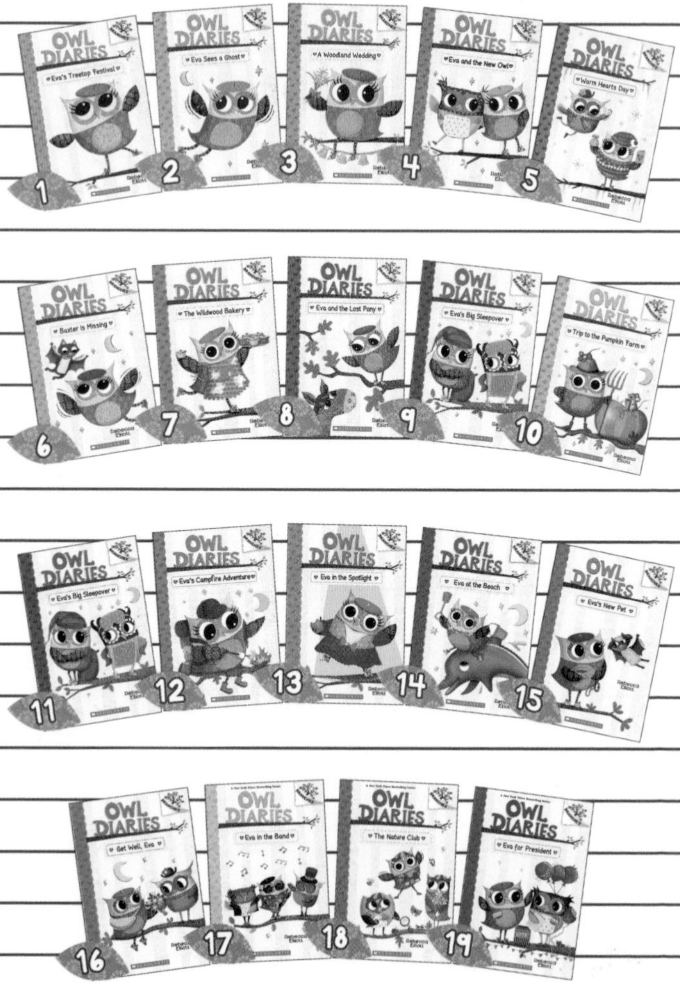

1 Eva's Treetop Festival
2 Eva Sees a Ghost
3 A Woodland Wedding
4 Eva and the New Owl
5 Warm Hearts Day
6 Baxter Is Missing
7 The Wildwood Bakery
8 Eva and the Lost Pony
9 Eva's Big Sleepover
10 Trip to the Pumpkin Farm
11 Eva's Big Sleepover
12 Eva's Campfire Adventure
13 Eva in the Spotlight
14 Eva at the Beach
15 Eva's New Pet
16 Get Well, Eva
17 Eva in the Band
18 The Nature Club
19 Eva for President

OWL DIARIES

♡ The Nature Club ♡

Rebecca
Elliott

BRANCHES

SCHOLASTIC INC.

For Clementine, who always loved
a walk in the woods. X.—R.E.

Special thanks to Collaborate Agency for
their contributions to this book.

Library of Congress Cataloging-in-Publication Data
Names: Elliott, Rebecca, author, illustrator.
Title: The nature club / Rebecca Elliott.
Description: First edition | New York : Branches/Scholastic, Inc., 2023. |
Series: Owl diaries ; 18 | Audience: Ages 5–7. | Audience: Grades K–2. |
Summary: When Mrs. Featherbottom places Eva in a different club from
Lucy and Hailey, Eva misses her best friends, but she learns new things
about her classmates, and discovers that someone in her
club is missing a friend, too.
Identifiers: LCCN 2022041071 (print) | LCCN 2022041072 (ebook) |
ISBN 9781338745467 (paperback) | ISBN 9781338745474 (library binding) |
ISBN 9781338745481 (ebk)
Subjects: CYAC: Owls—Fiction. | Best friends—Fiction. |
Friendship—Fiction. | Nature—Fiction. | Schools—Fiction. |
Diaries--Fiction. | BISAC: JUVENILE FICTION / Readers / Chapter Books |
JUVENILE FICTION / Animals / Birds | LCGFT: Animal fiction.
Classification: LCC PZ7.E45812 Nat 2023 (print) | LCC PZ7.E45812 (ebook)
| DDC [Fic]—dc23
LC record available at https://lccn.loc.gov/2022041071

ISBN 978-1-338-74547-4 (hardcover) / ISBN 978-1-338-74546-7 (paperback)

10 9 8 7 6 5 4 3 2 1   22 23 24 25 26

Printed in China   62
First edition, May 2023

Edited by Katie Carella and Alli Brydon
Book design by Marissa Asuncion

♡ Table of Contents ♡

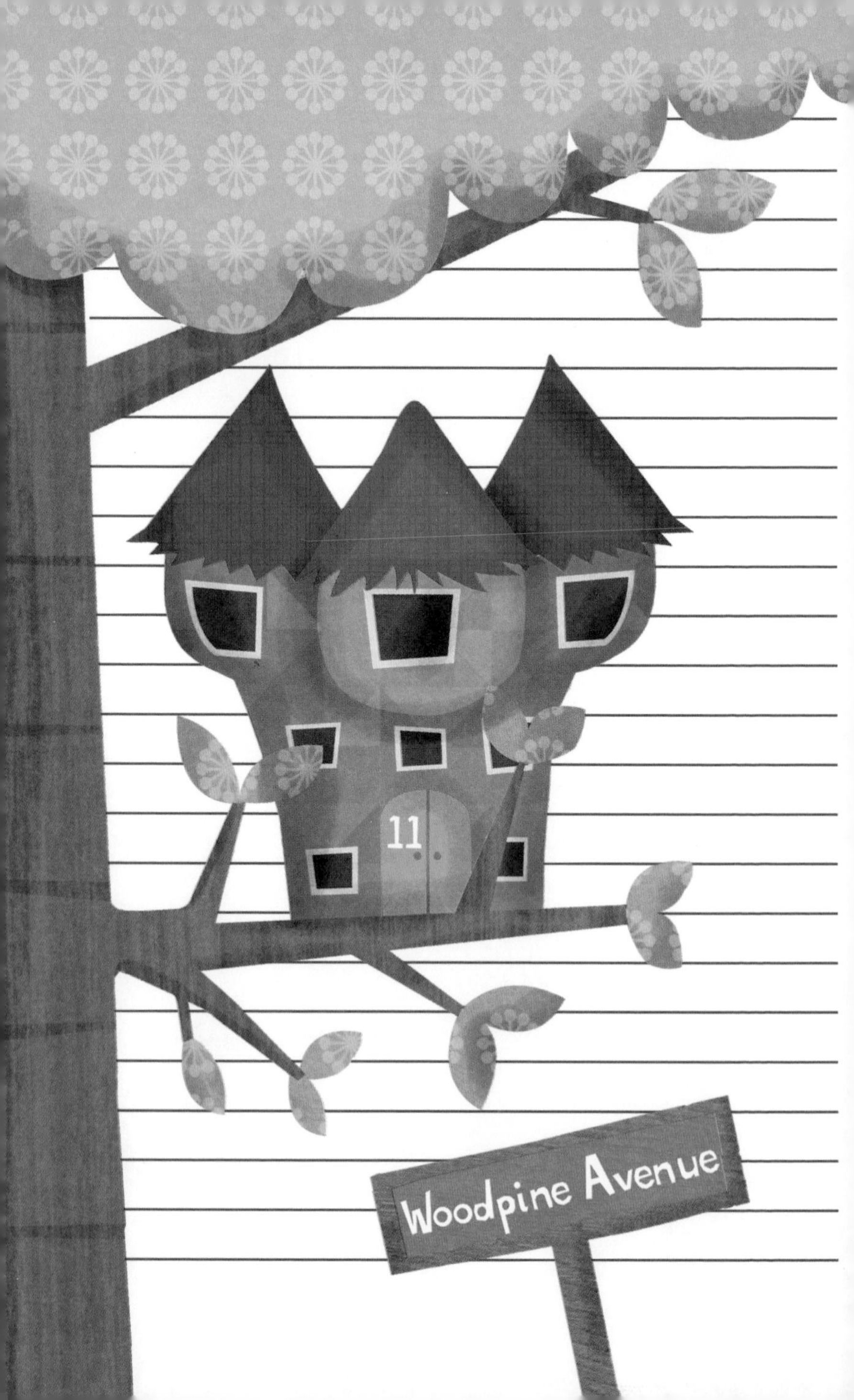

11
Woodpine Avenue

1

Nature Day

Sunday

Hello, Diary!

It's me, Eva. Next Saturday is Nature Day! There is going to be a party at the Old Oak Tree to celebrate the planet.

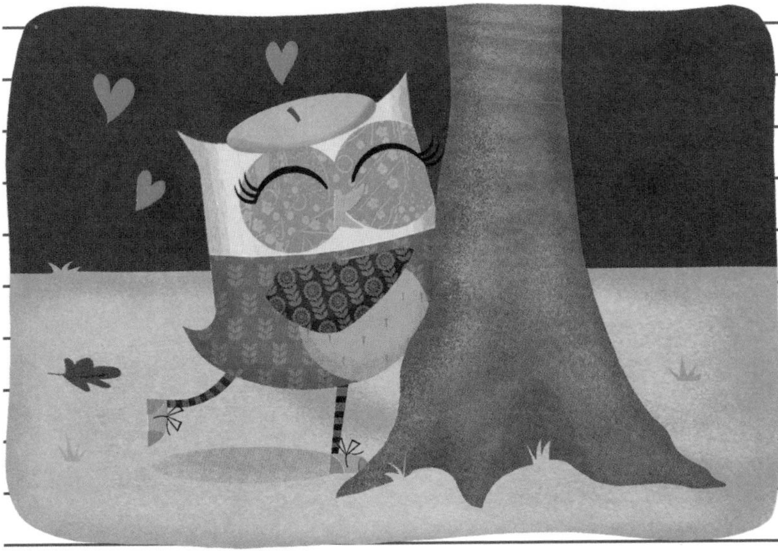

I love:

Nature!

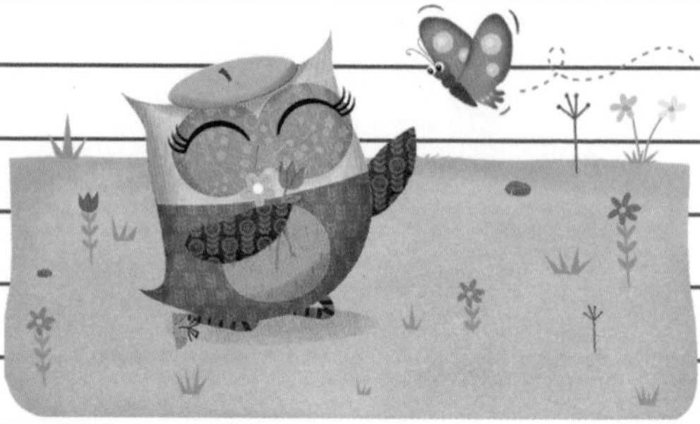

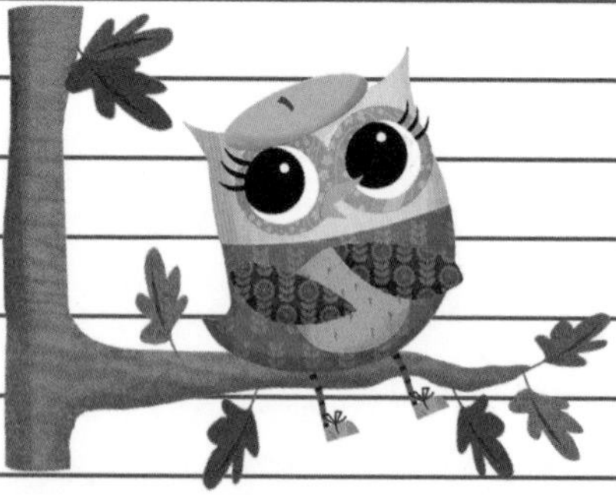

Leafy trees

Finding bugs outside

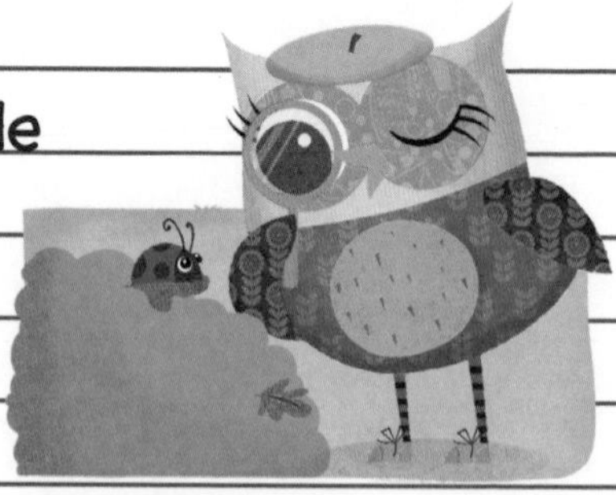

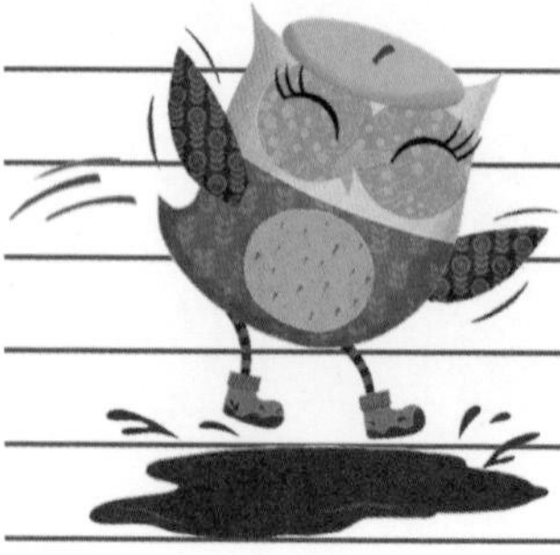

Splashing in puddles

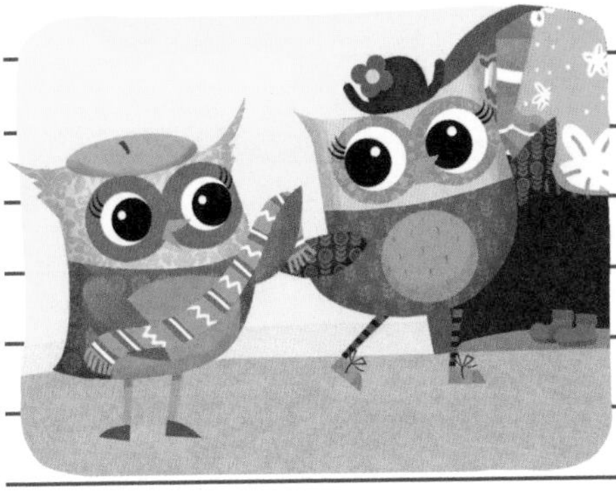

Swapping . . .
instead of
shopping!

Planting seeds

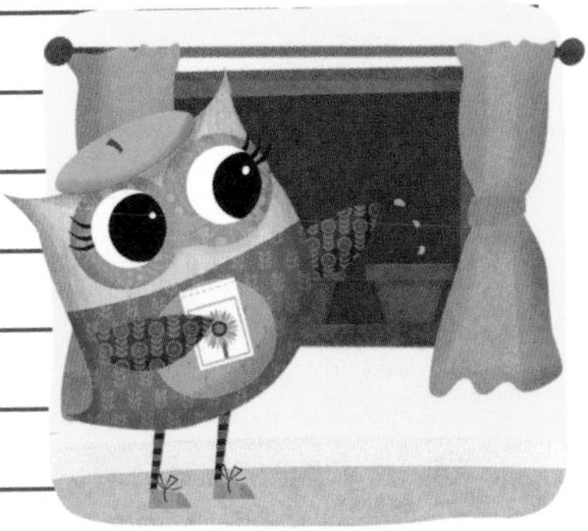

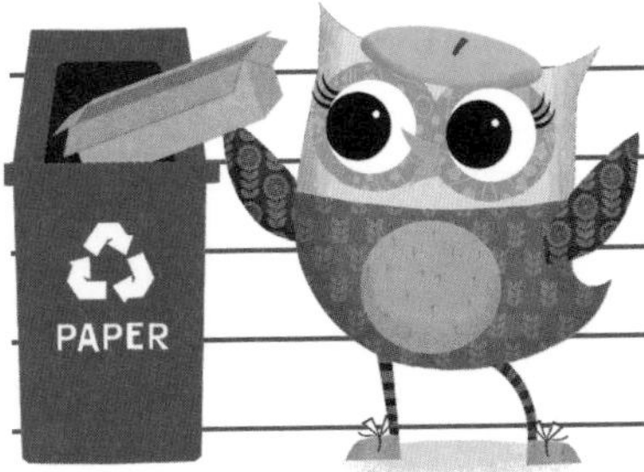
PAPER

Recycling boxes

The word Earth

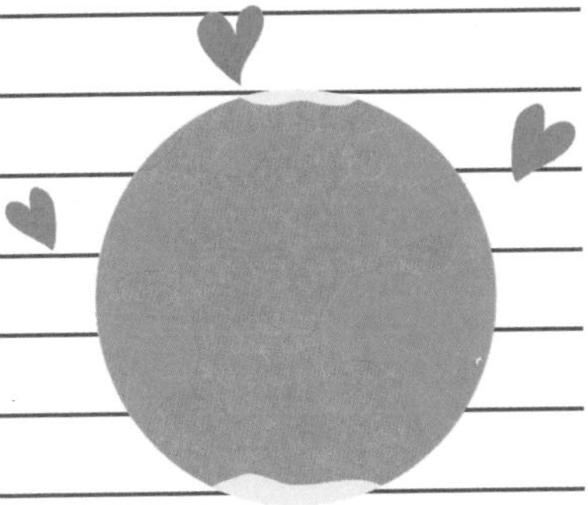

I DO NOT love:

Litter

Seeing nature
get hurt

Crashing into
leafy trees

Finding bugs
inside

4

Holes in my rain boots

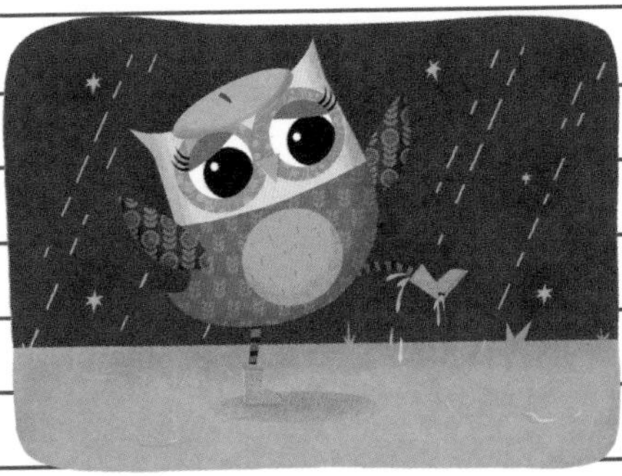

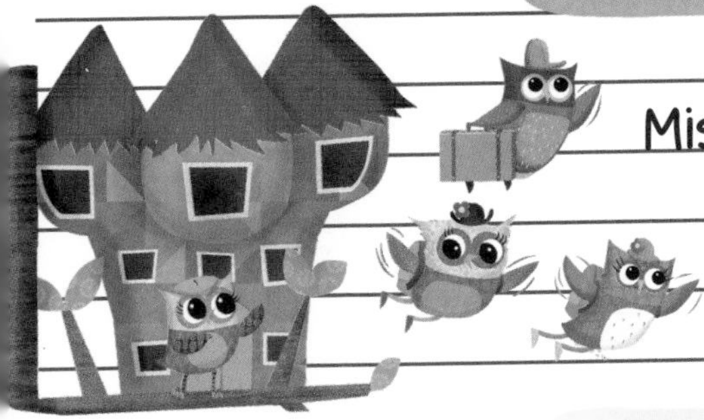

Missing my BFF

Forgetting to water my plants

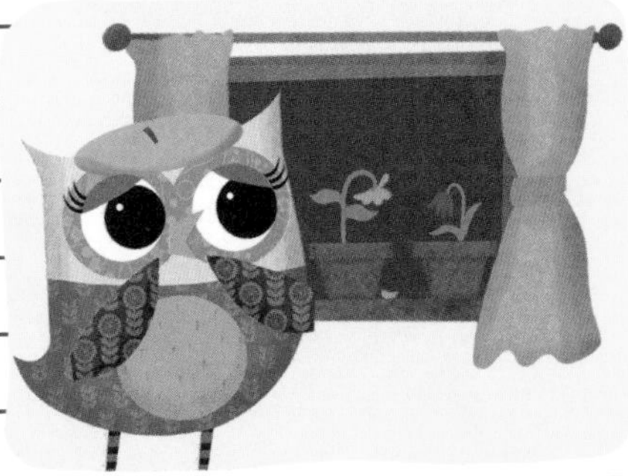

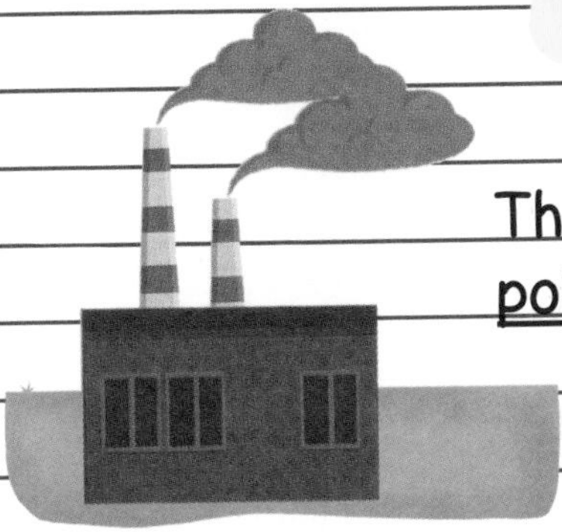

The word <u>pollution</u>

This is my **WING-CREDIBLE** family.

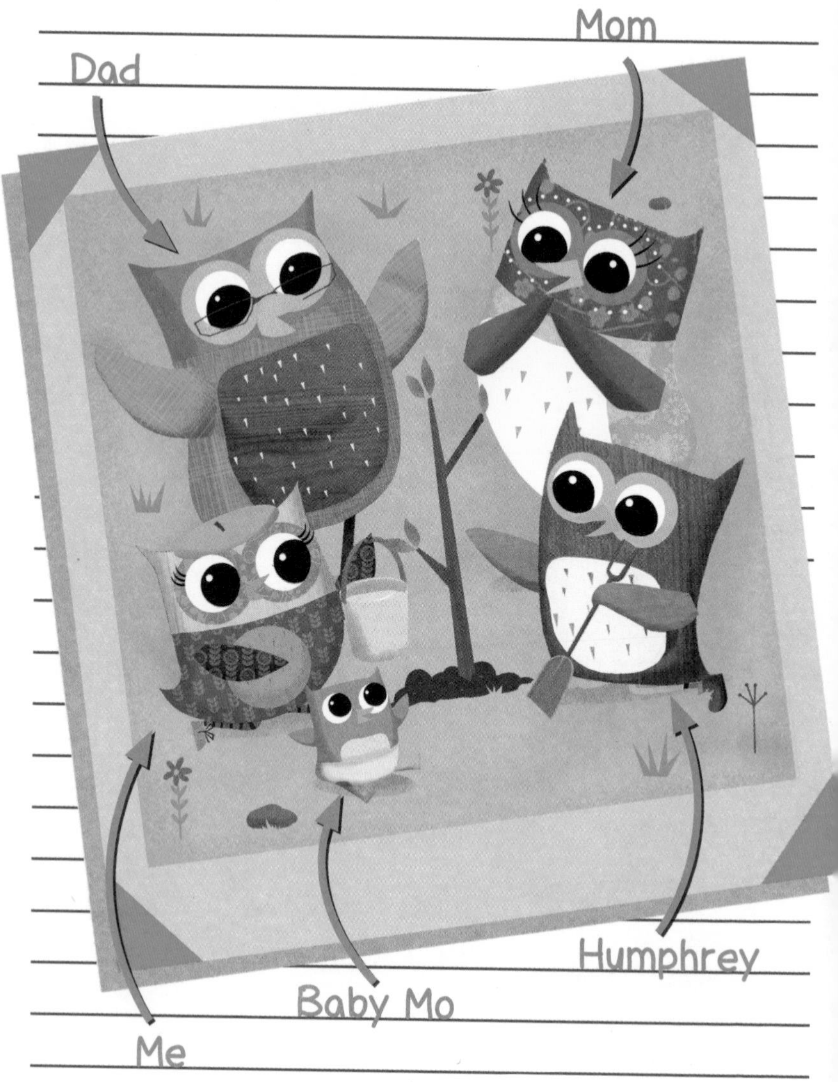

Mom
Dad
Humphrey
Baby Mo
Me

And these are my pets, Baxter the bat and Acorn the flying squirrel. They love nature, too!

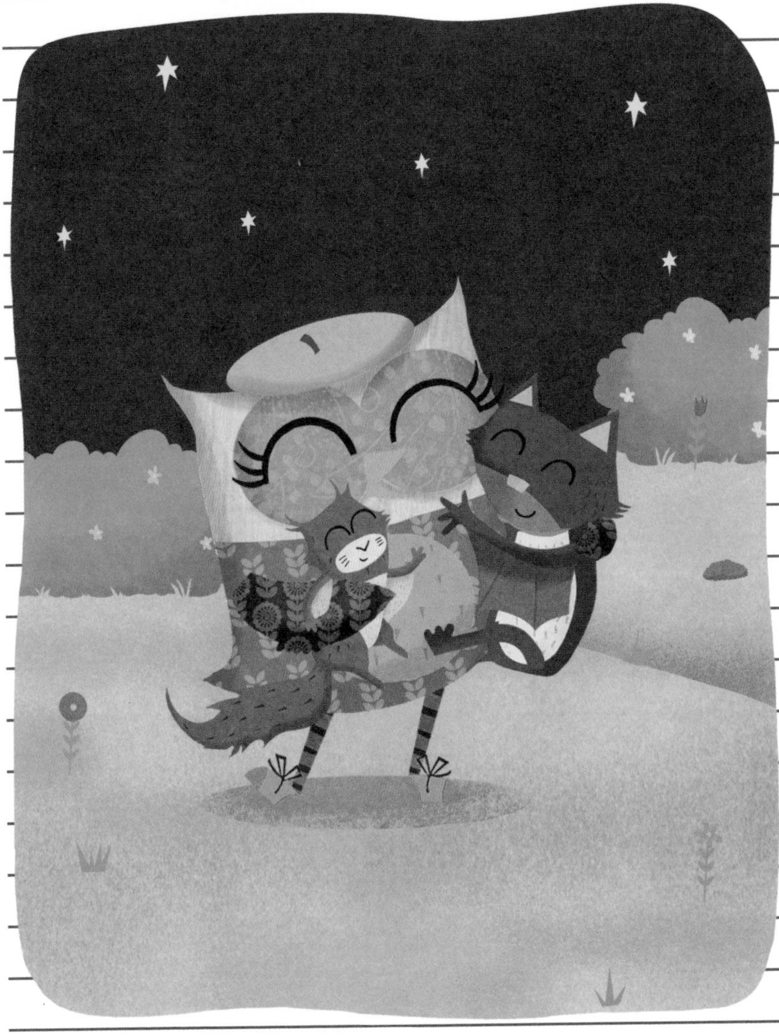

Being an owl is **FLAPPY-FABULOUS**.

We're awake at night instead of during the day.

We can stretch, yawn, and comb our heads.

We can swim!

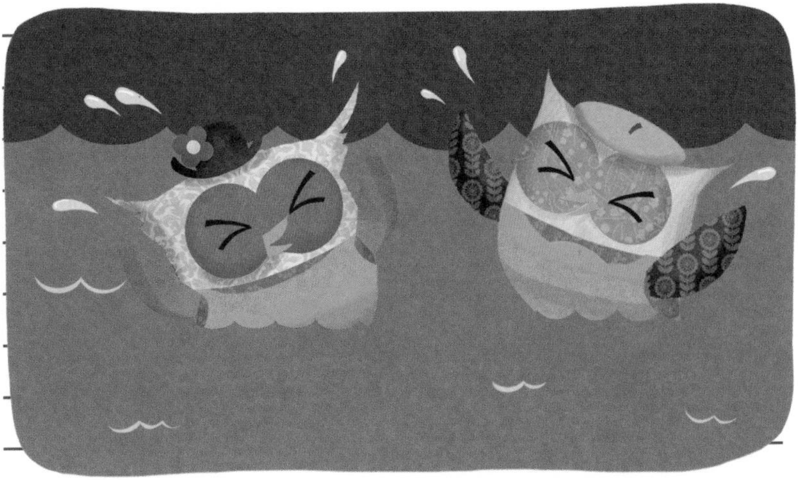

The biggest owl in the world has a wingspan as wide as a couch!

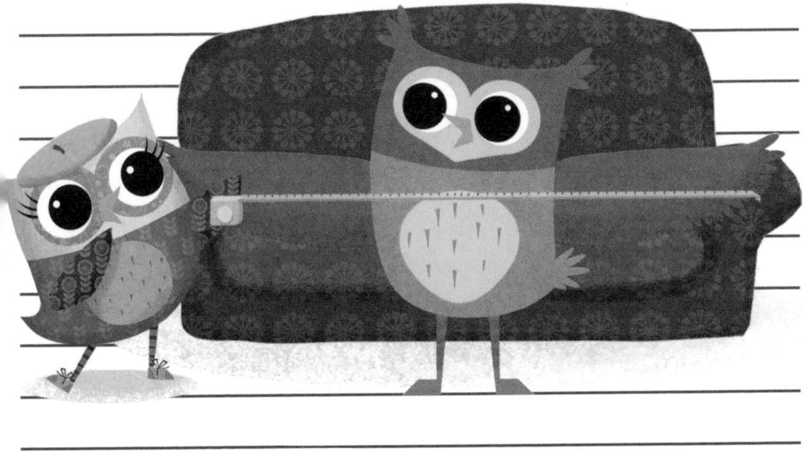

My address is 11 Woodpine Avenue, Treetopolis, Planet Earth. My BFF (**BEST FEATHERY FRIEND**), Lucy, lives next door.

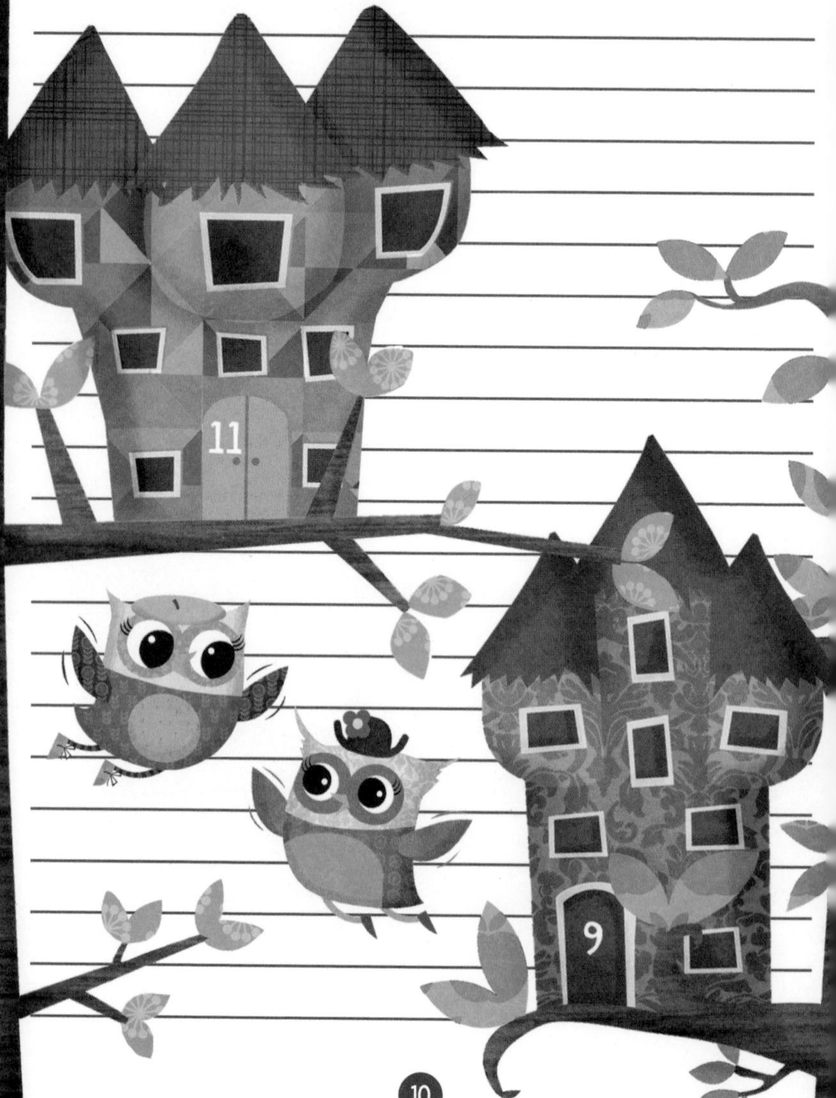
11
9

We go to Treetop Owlementary School. Here's our class:

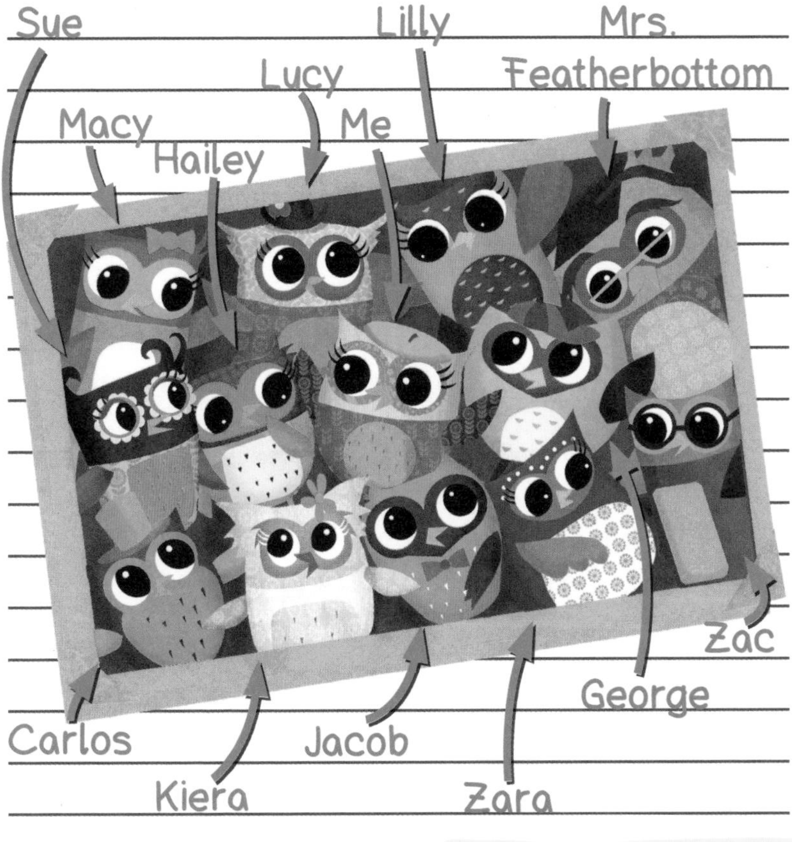

Sue
Lilly
Mrs. Featherbottom
Lucy
Macy
Me
Hailey
Zac
George
Carlos
Jacob
Kiera
Zara

ANYHOOT, I can't wait for tomorrow – because it's one day closer to Nature Day!

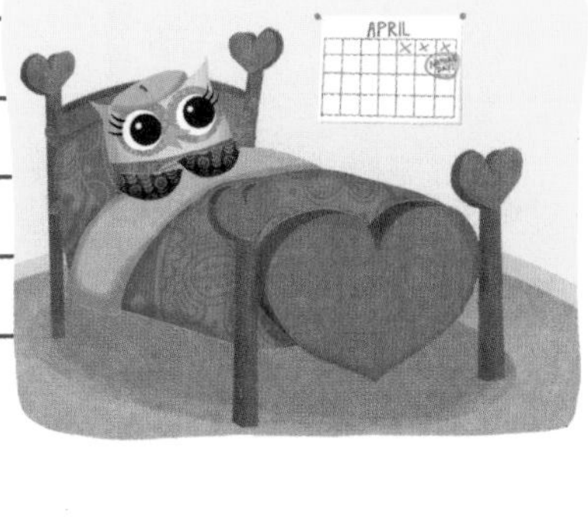

APRIL

2

Mission: Save the Planet!

Monday

At school this week, we'll be learning about nature. Tonight, Mrs. Featherbottom talked about how important it is to love and protect our planet.

We only have one Earth. We must look after it!

Then she announced a cool project.

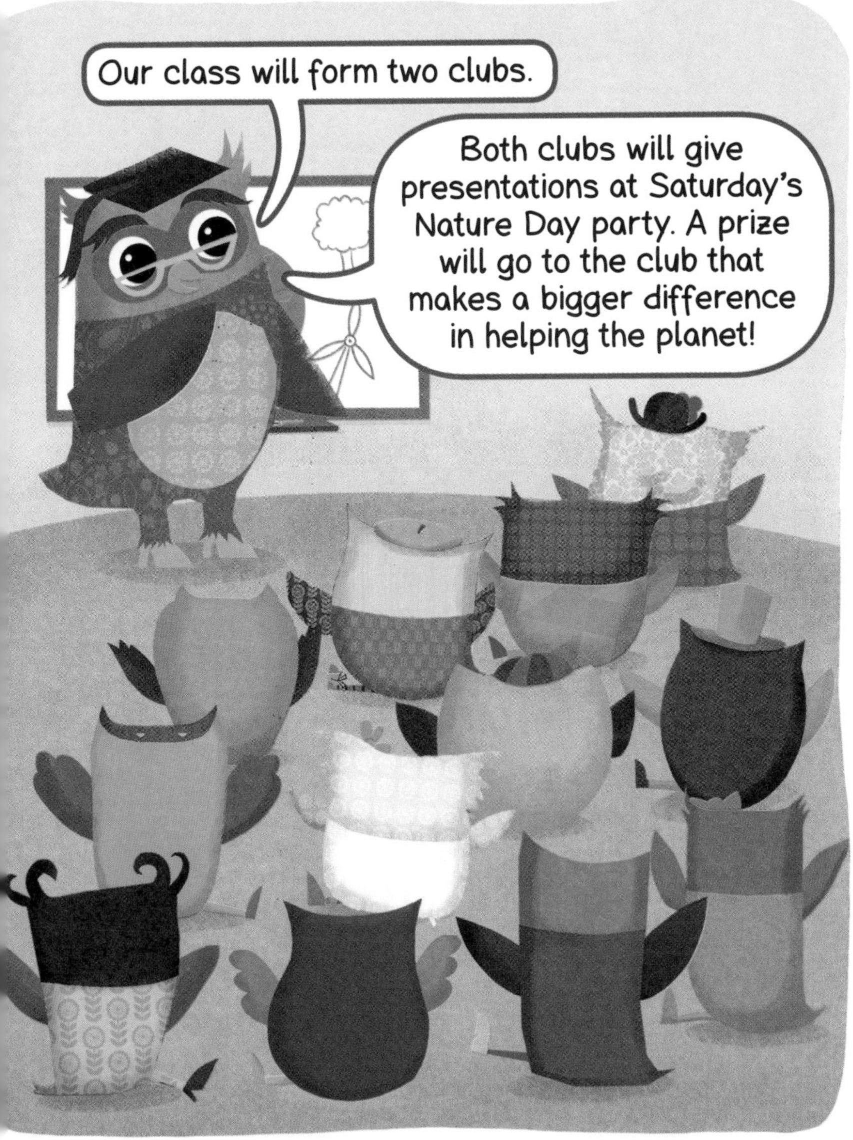
Our class will form two clubs.
Both clubs will give presentations at Saturday's Nature Day party. A prize will go to the club that makes a bigger difference in helping the planet!

We were all buzzing with excitement.

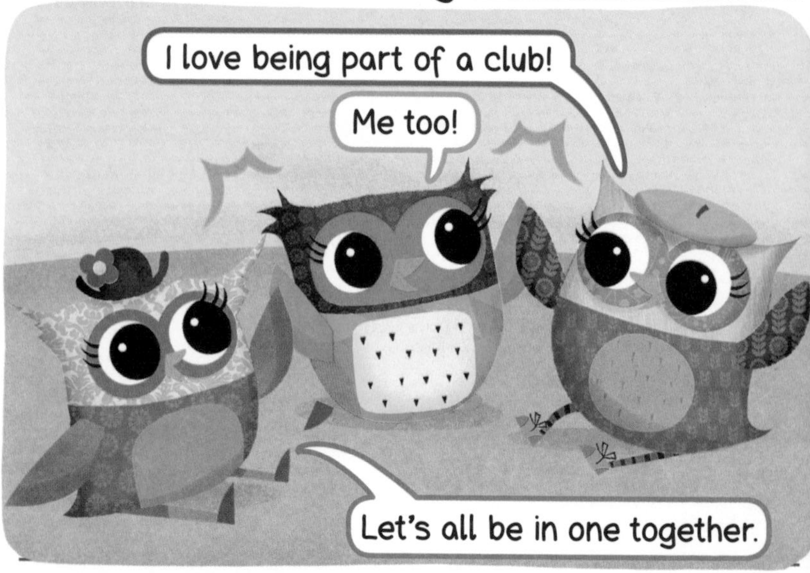
I love being part of a club!
Me too!
Let's all be in one together.

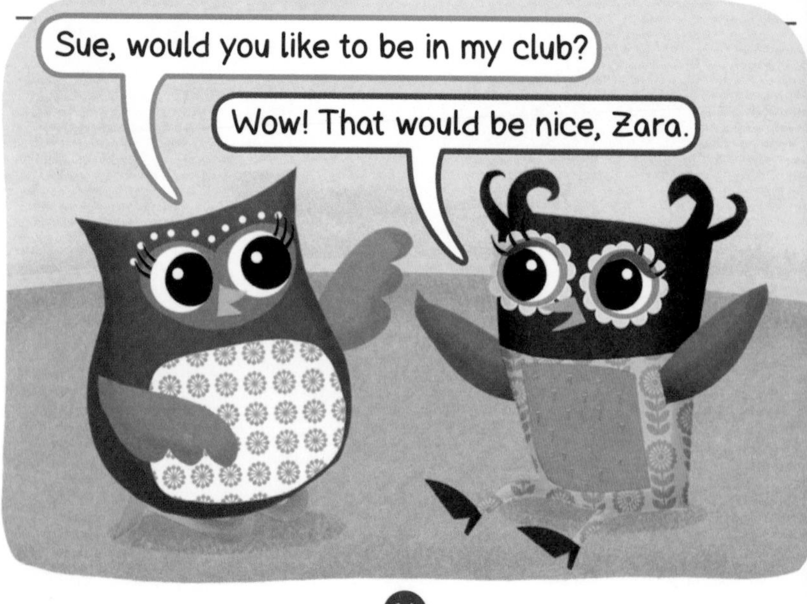
Sue, would you like to be in my club?
Wow! That would be nice, Zara.

But then Mrs. Featherbottom said something surprising.

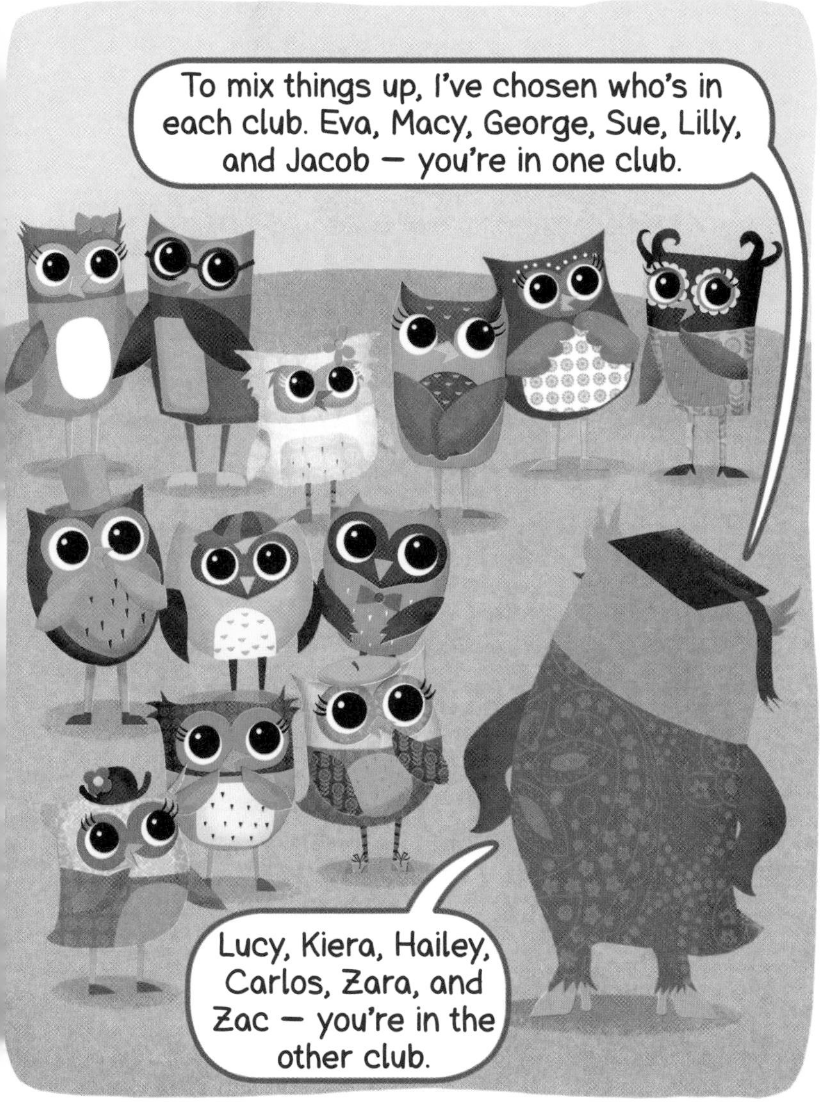
To mix things up, I've chosen who's in each club. Eva, Macy, George, Sue, Lilly, and Jacob — you're in one club.
Lucy, Kiera, Hailey, Carlos, Zara, and Zac — you're in the other club.

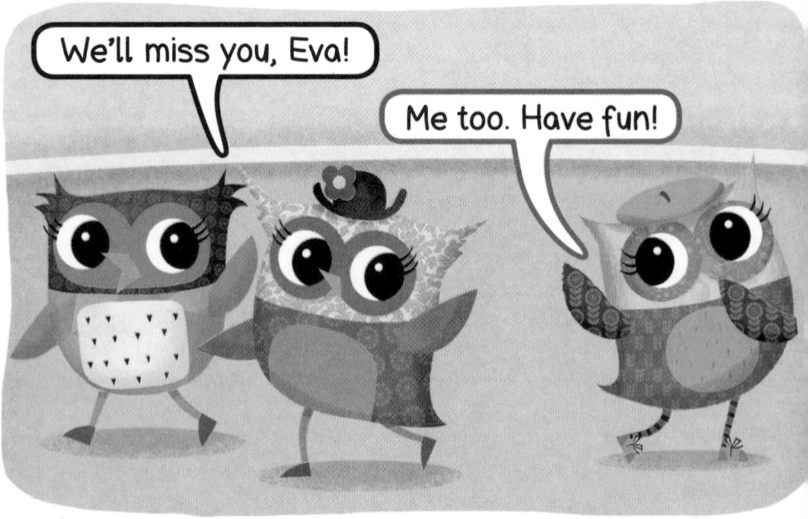
We'll miss you, Eva!
Me too. Have fun!

I wanted to work with my BFFs, Lucy and Hailey. But I was also excited about being in a new club.

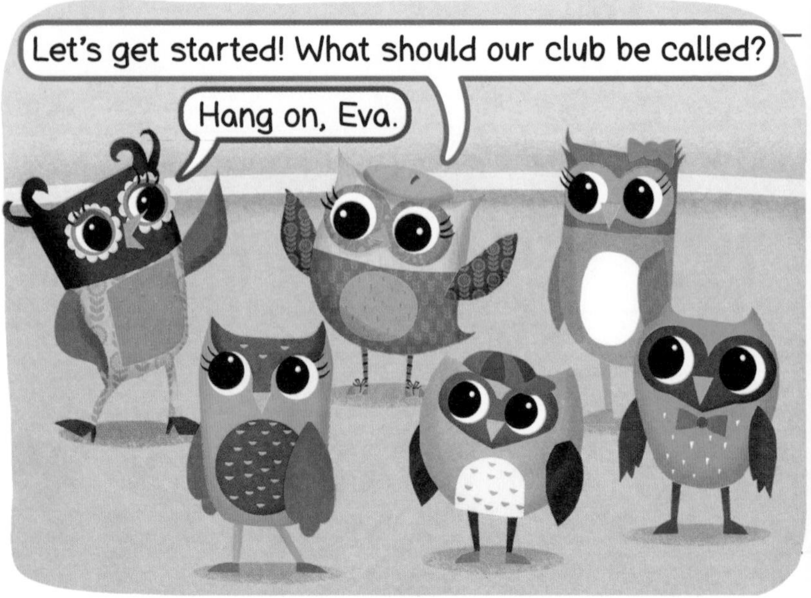
Let's get started! What should our club be called?
Hang on, Eva.

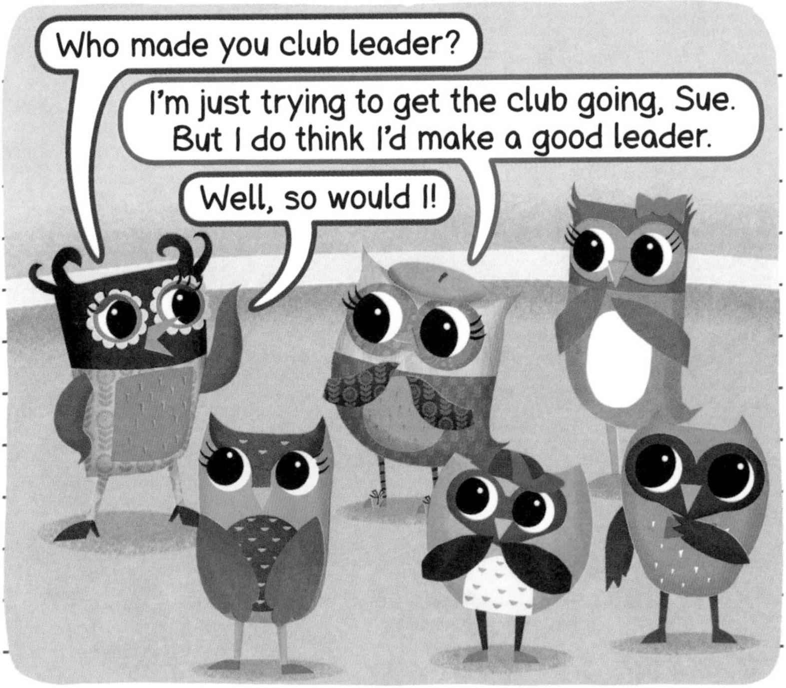
Who made you club leader?
I'm just trying to get the club going, Sue. But I do think I'd make a good leader.
Well, so would I!

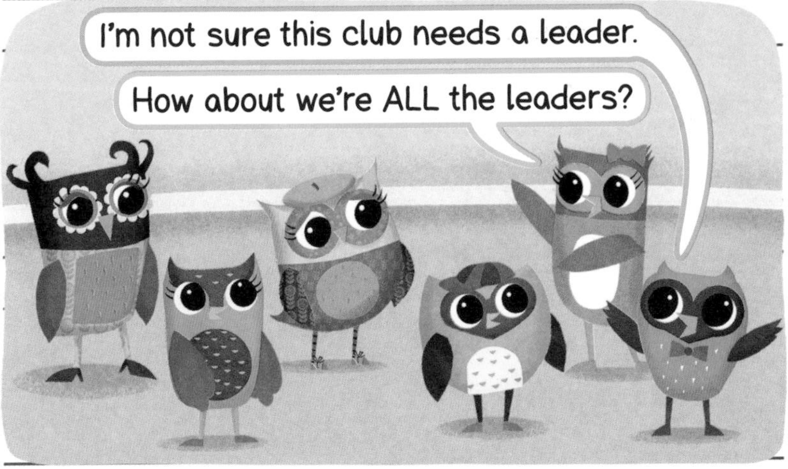
I'm not sure this club needs a leader.
How about we're ALL the leaders?

In the end, we agreed we would <u>all</u> be the leaders.

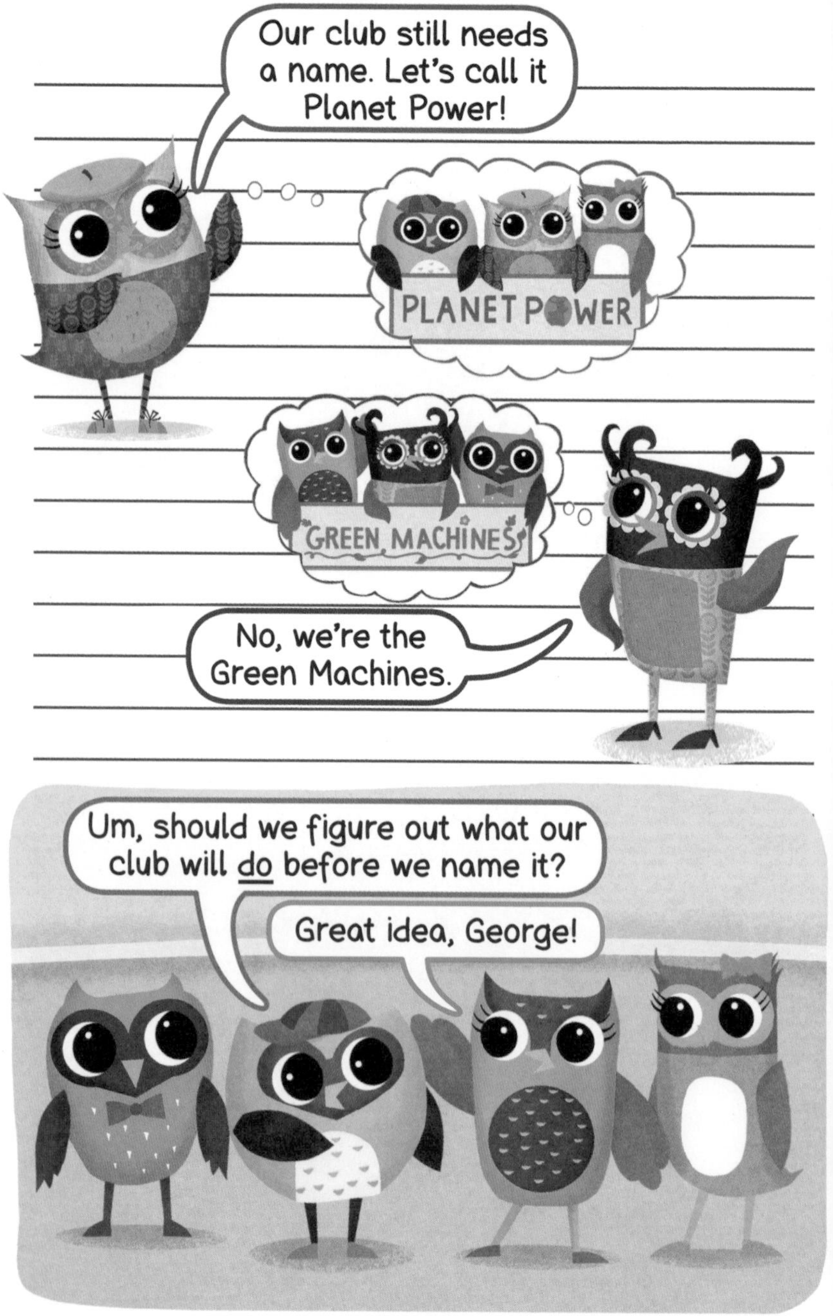
Our club still needs a name. Let's call it Planet Power!
PLANET POWER
GREEN MACHINES
No, we're the Green Machines.
Um, should we figure out what our club will do before we name it?
Great idea, George!

To help the planet, we decided to start with our home – the forest.

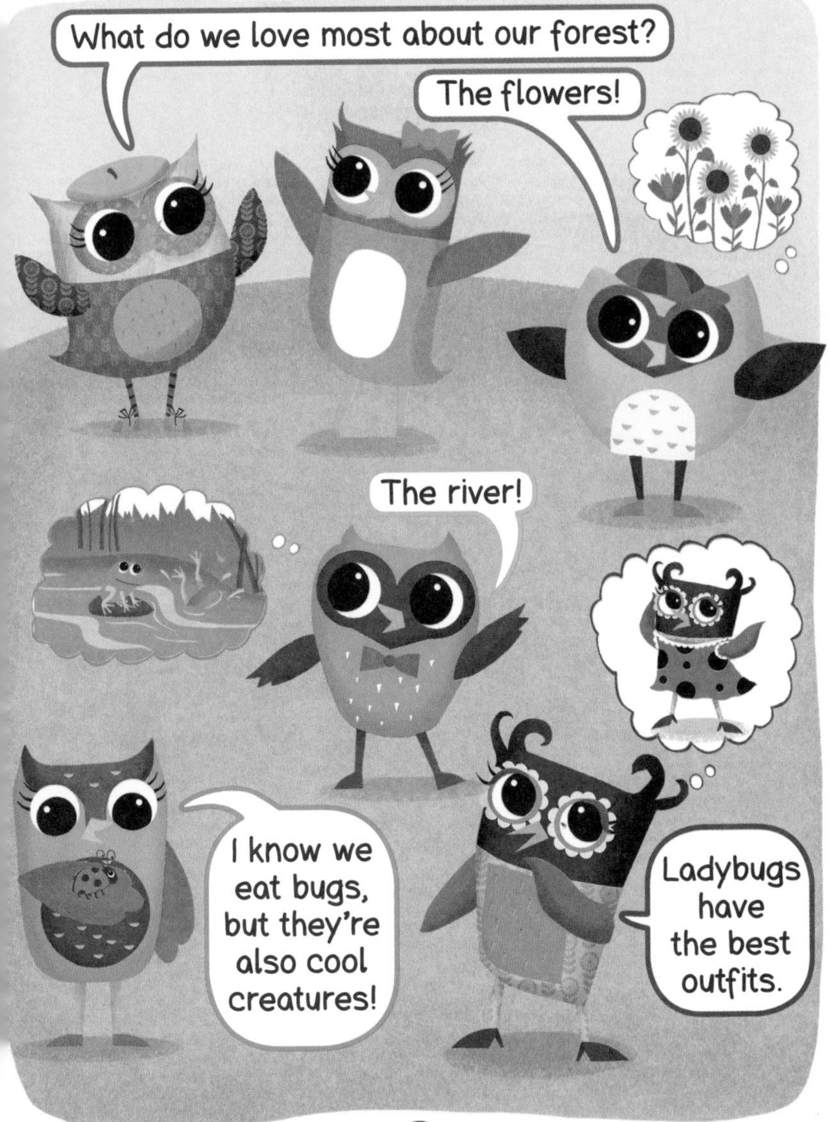

What do we love most about our forest?
The flowers!
The river!
I know we eat bugs, but they're also cool creatures!
Ladybugs have the best outfits.

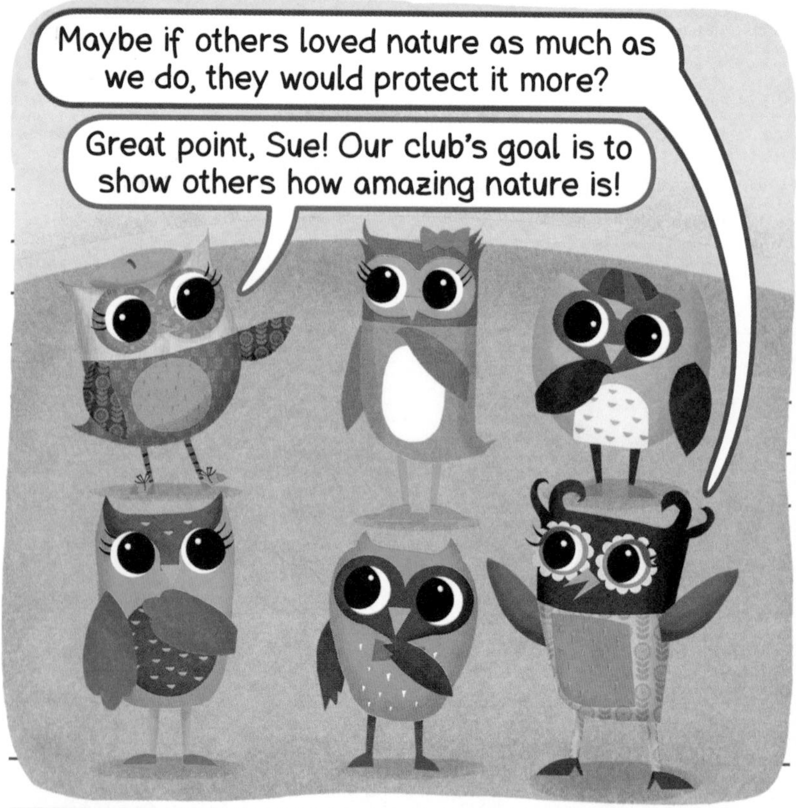
Maybe if others loved nature as much as we do, they would protect it more?
Great point, Sue! Our club's goal is to show others how amazing nature is!

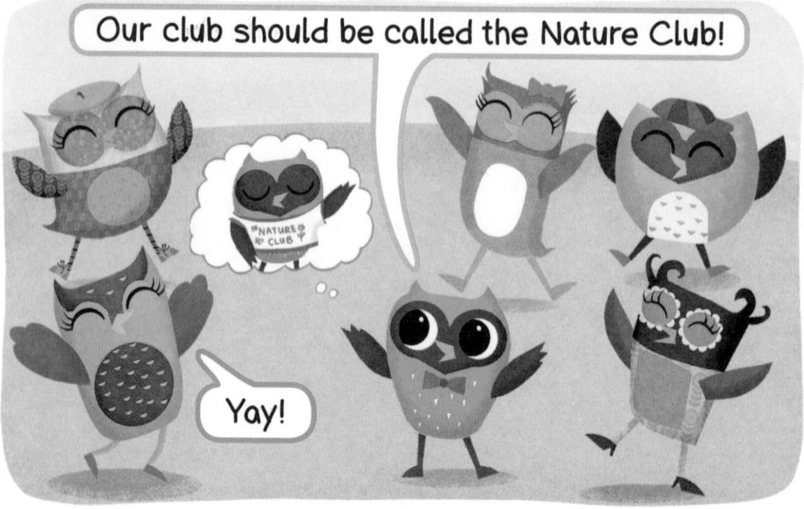
Our club should be called the Nature Club!
NATURE CLUB
Yay!

After school, Lucy came over to my tree house. I told her about our club's goal.

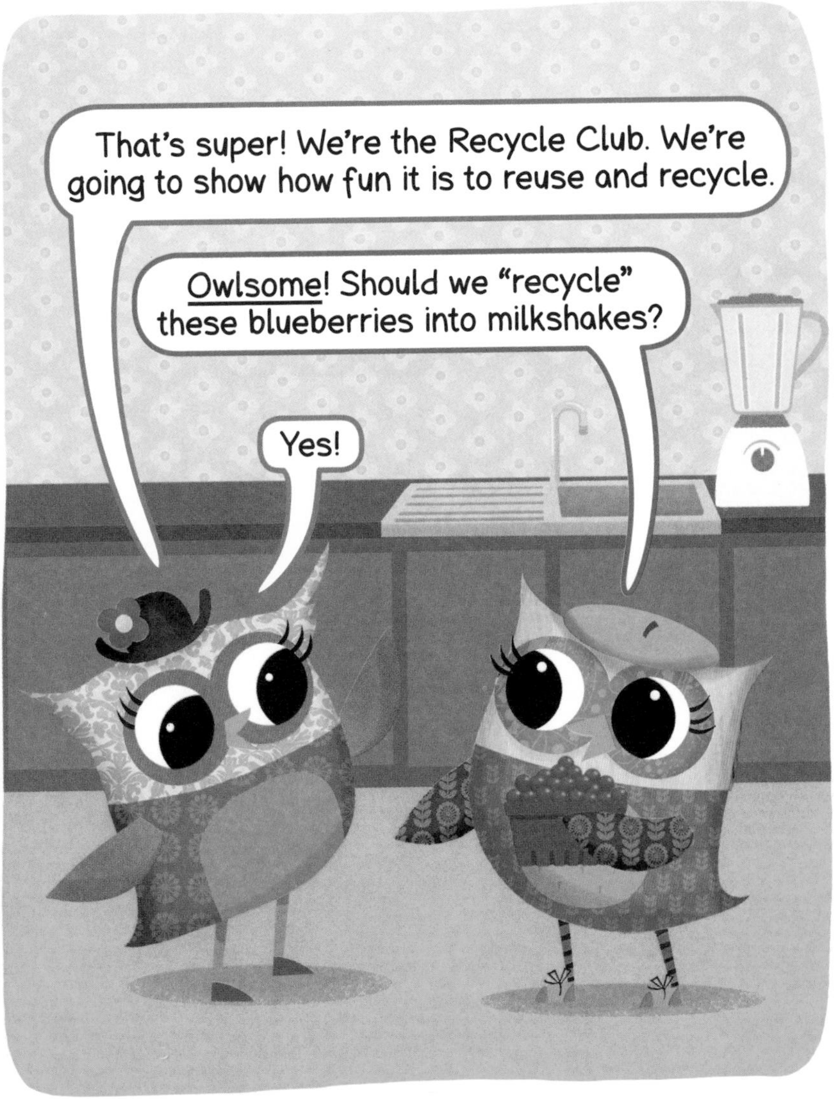
That's super! We're the Recycle Club. We're going to show how fun it is to reuse and recycle.
Owlsome! Should we "recycle" these blueberries into milkshakes?
Yes!

We made yummy milkshakes!

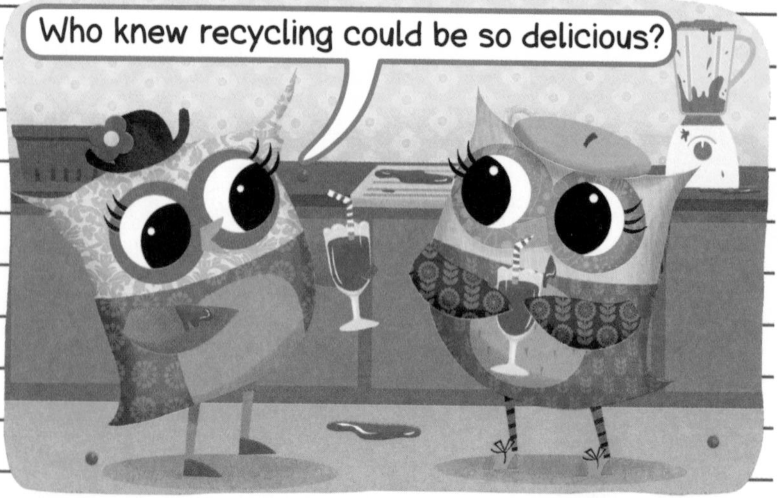
Who knew recycling could be so delicious?

I'm sad I'm not in the same club as Lucy, but at least we can still hang out after school. Time for bed, Diary . . . I have a planet to save tomorrow!

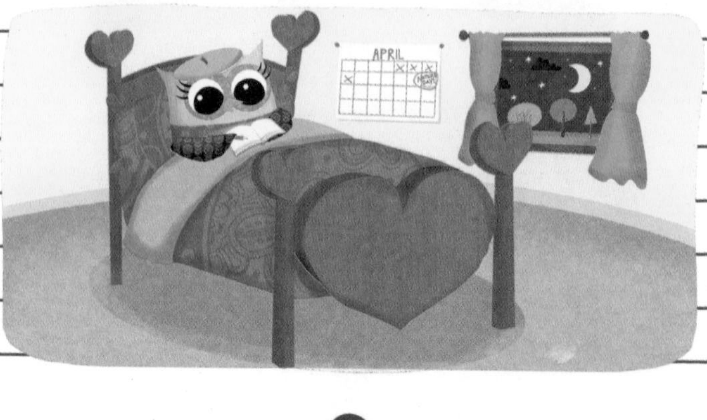
APRIL

♡ Hop In! ♡

Tuesday

School was a **HOOT** tonight! First, Mrs. Featherbottom gave us club hats!

Then we made club badges. What do you think, Diary?!

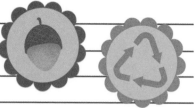

Next, Nature Club made a to-do list:

1. Plant flower seeds

2. Make posters about nature

PROTECT OUR PLANET!

3. Build a bug hotel

BUG HOTEL

4. Create wild art

But we couldn't agree on what we should do first!

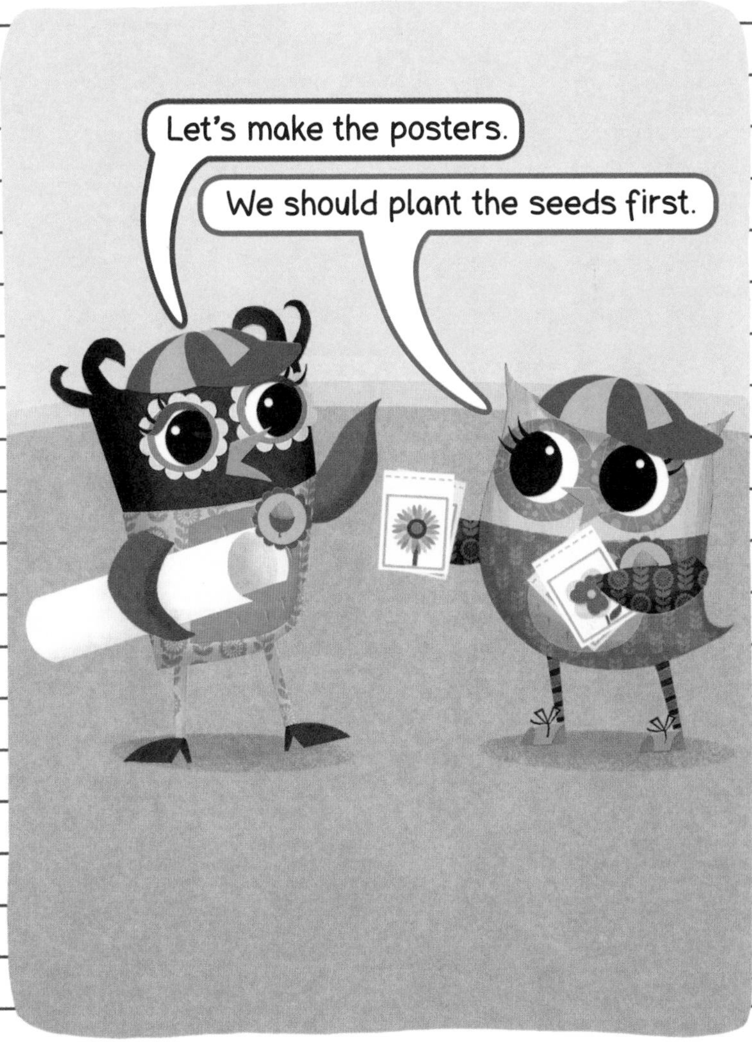
Let's make the posters.
We should plant the seeds first.

Mrs. Featherbottom flew over.

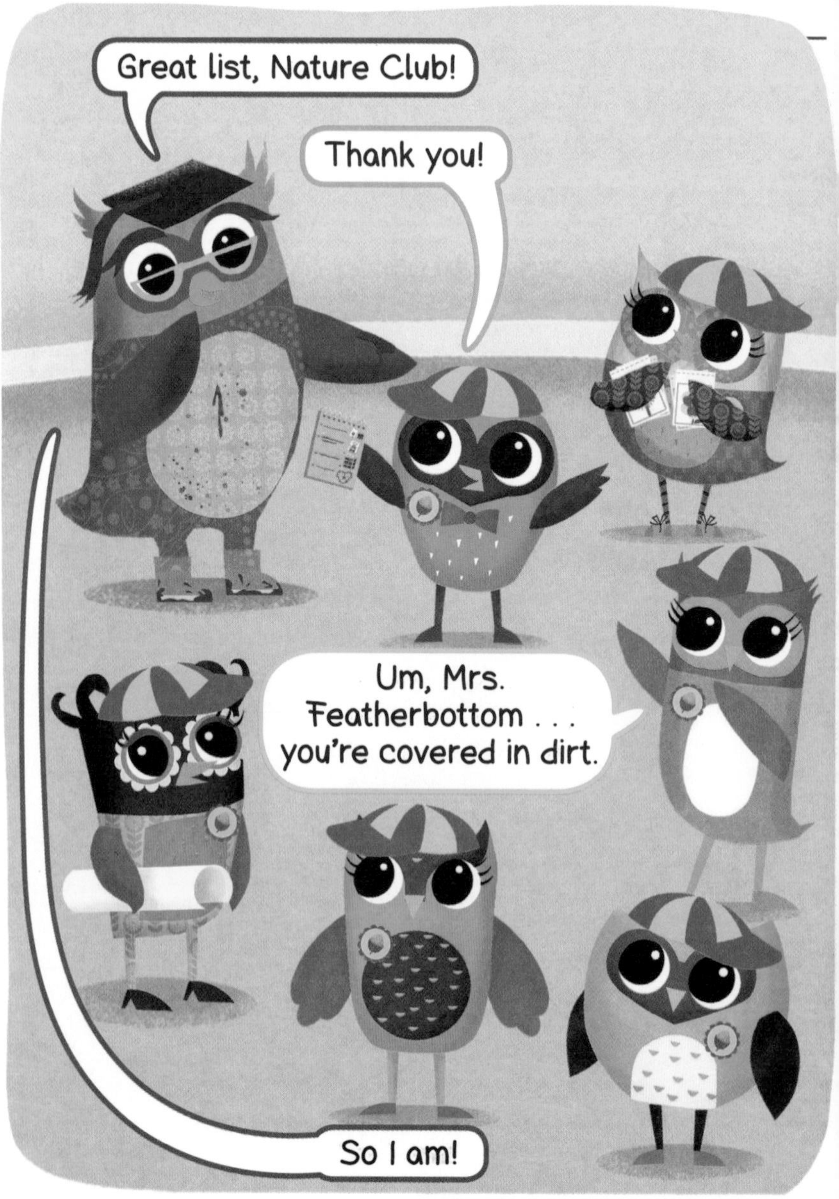

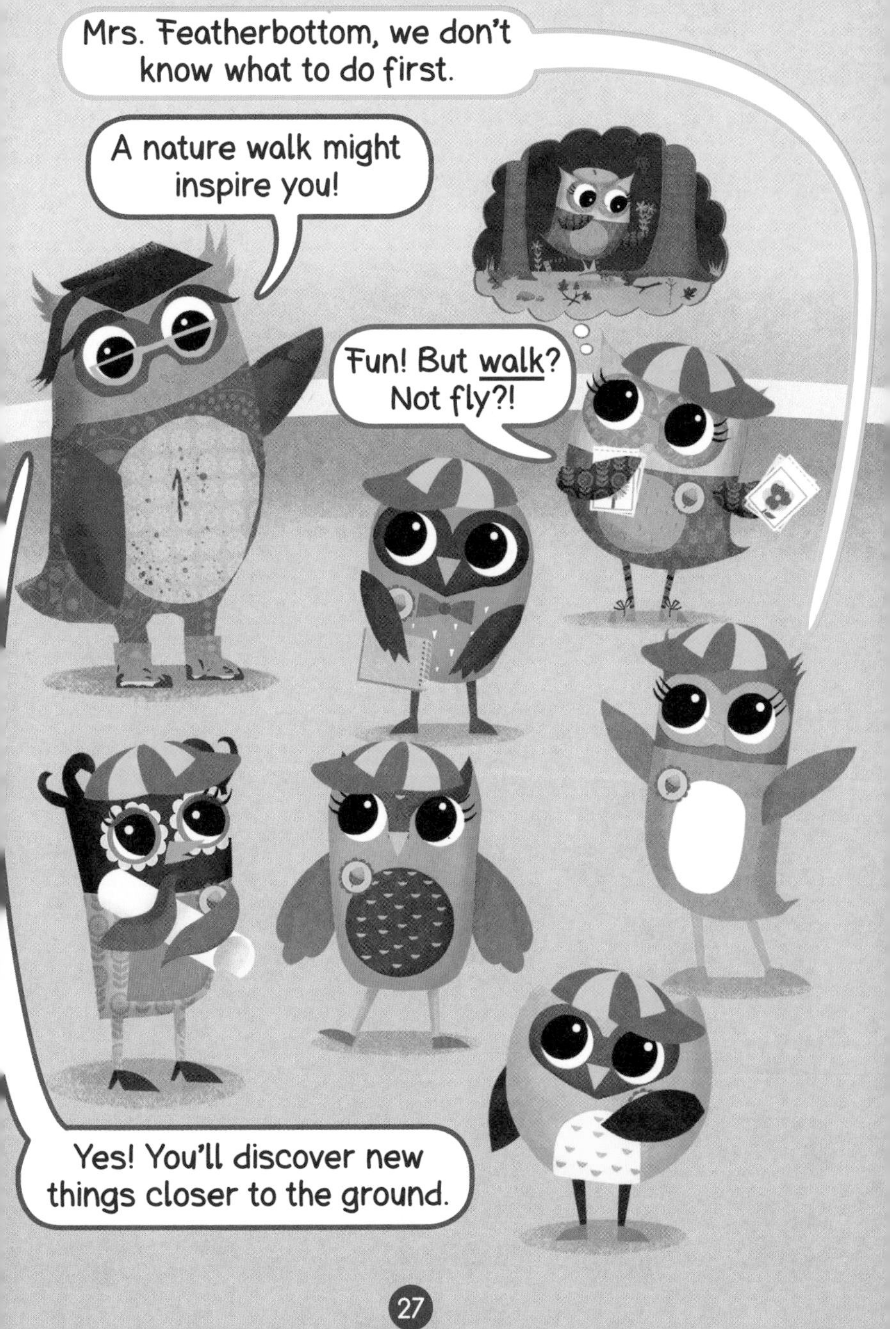
Mrs. Featherbottom, we don't know what to do first.
A nature walk might inspire you!
Fun! But walk? Not fly?!
Yes! You'll discover new things closer to the ground.

Our nature walk was **FLAPERRIFIC**! We discovered bugs. And we collected twigs, leaves, and pinecones to make our bug hotel and wild art.

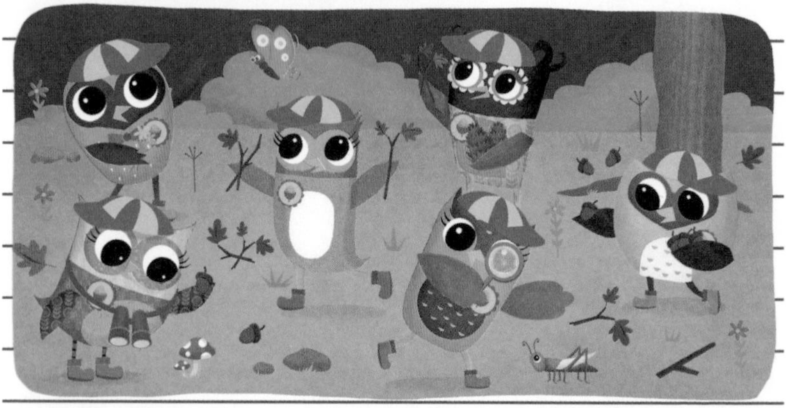

At the river, we saw lots of frogs!

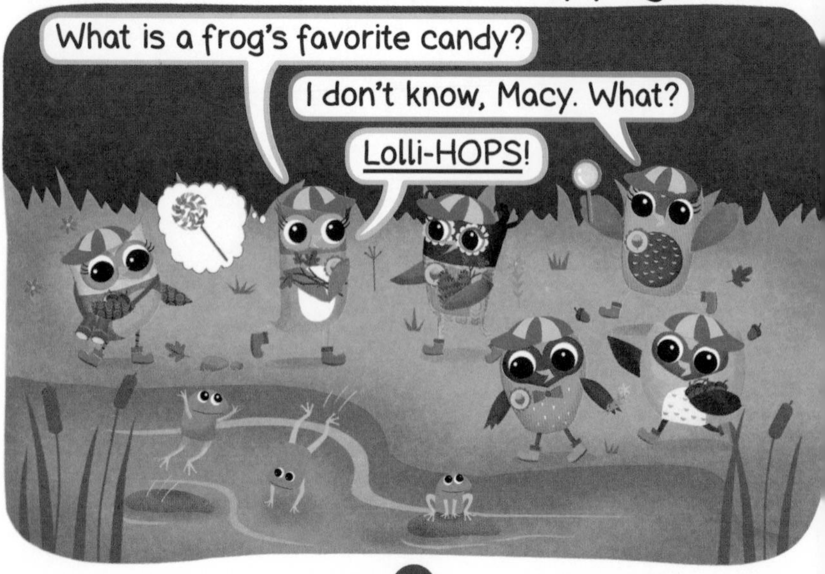
What is a frog's favorite candy?
I don't know, Macy. What?
Lolli-HOPS!

Then George noticed something **OWLFUL**. A frog was stuck in some trash!

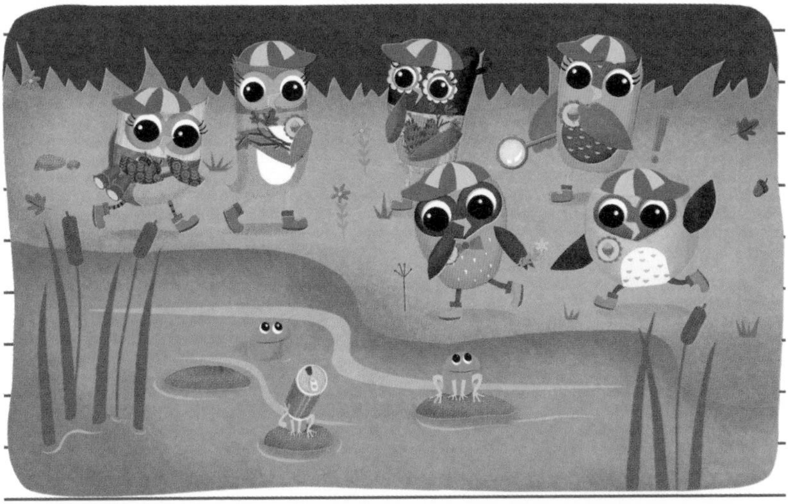

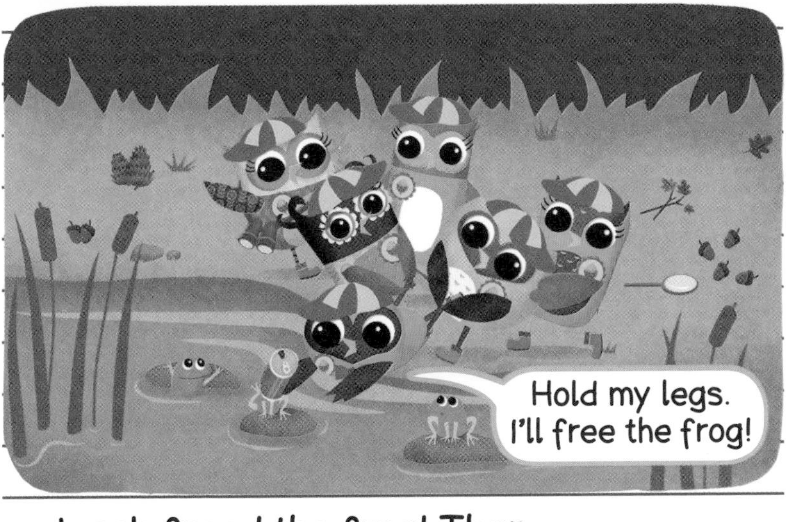
Hold my legs.
I'll free the frog!

Jacob freed the frog! Then —

He fell into the river!

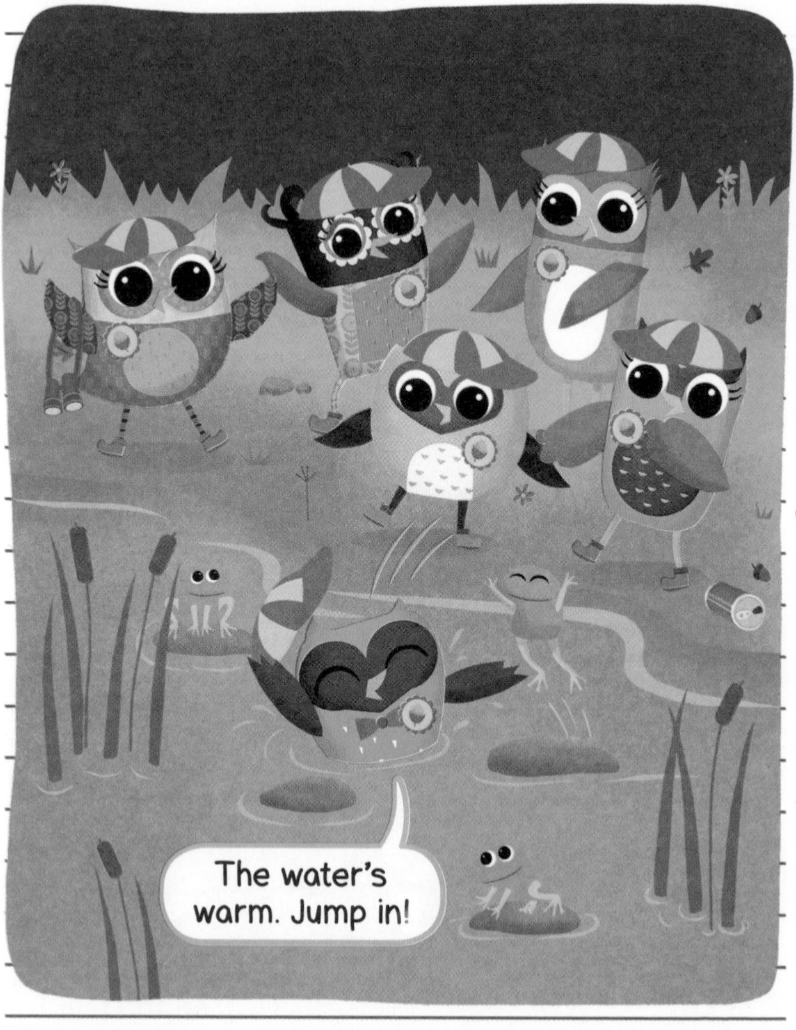
The water's
warm. Jump in!

We swam for a while. Then the Recycle Club flew by.

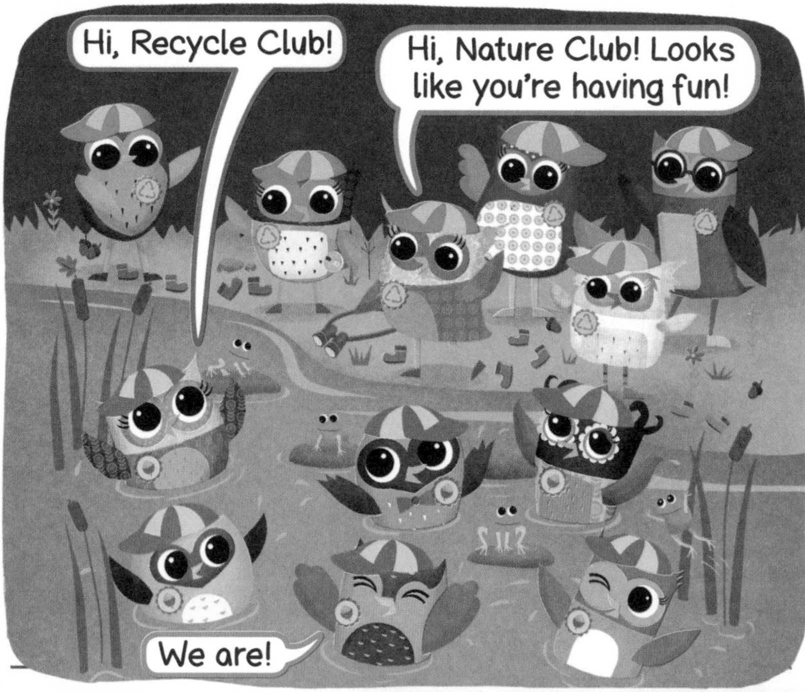
Hi, Recycle Club!
Hi, Nature Club! Looks like you're having fun!
We are!

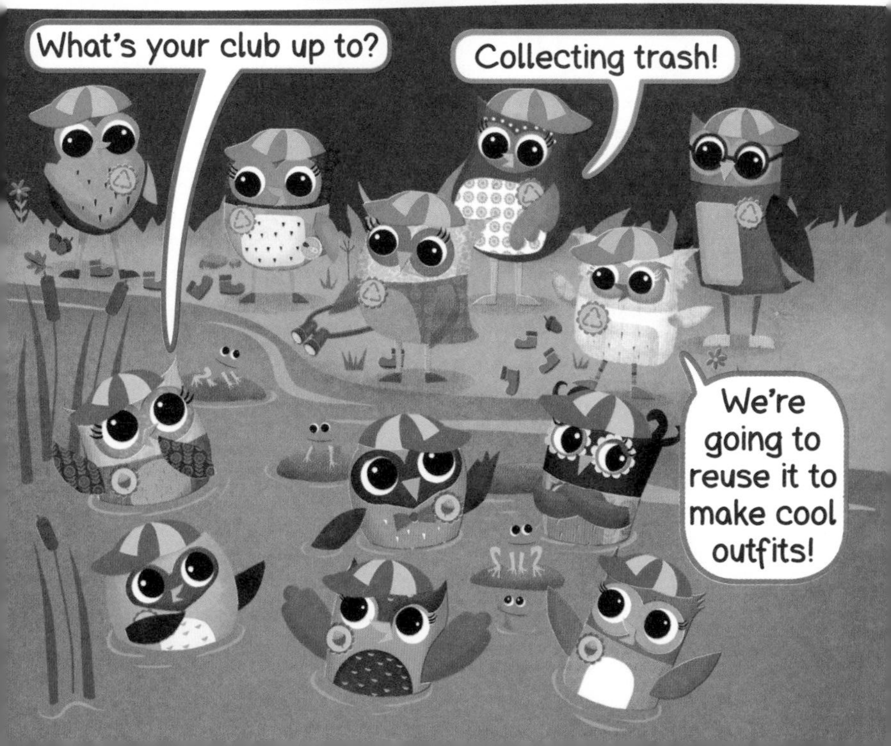
What's your club up to?
Collecting trash!
We're going to reuse it to make cool outfits!

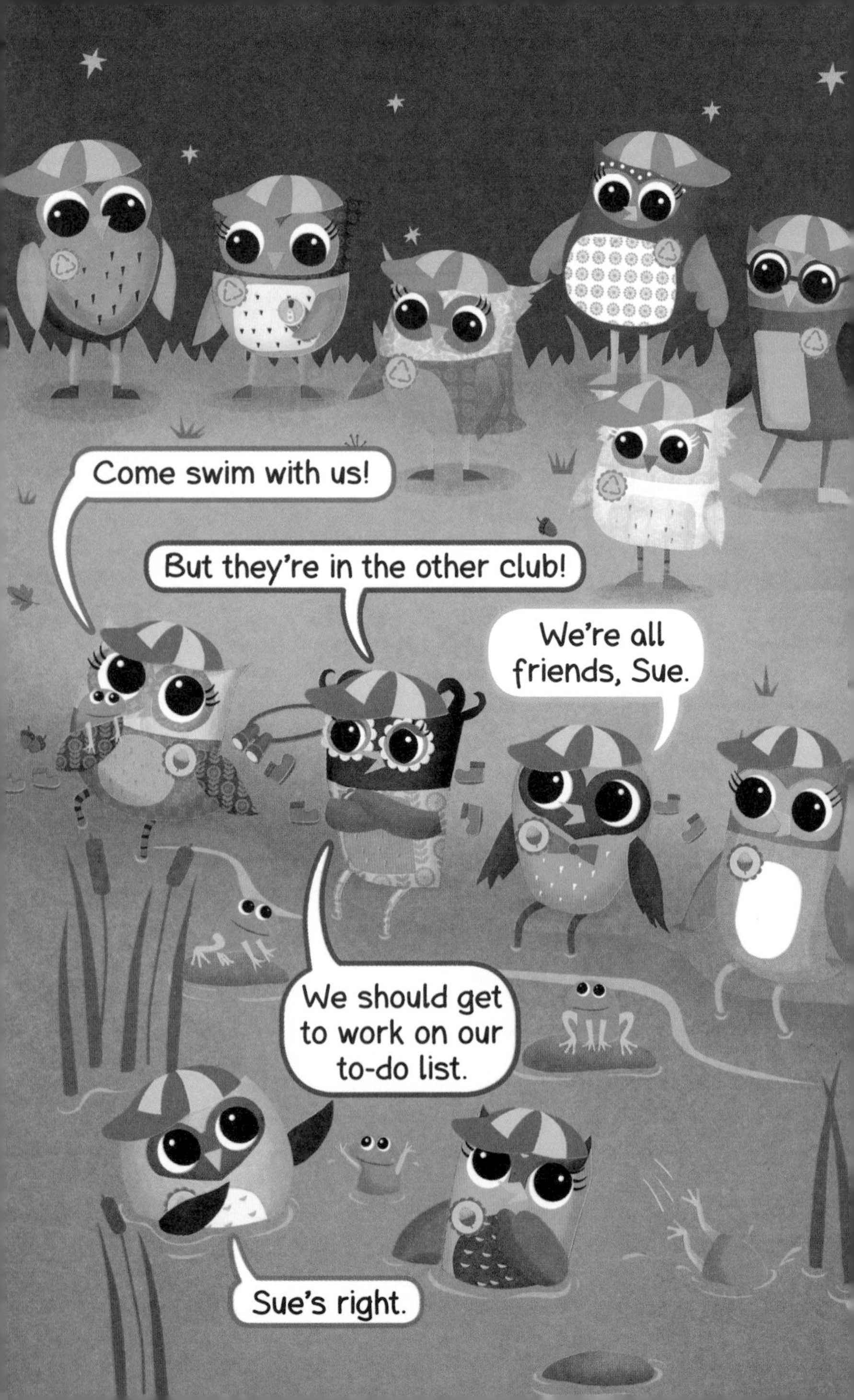
Come swim with us!
But they're in the other club!
We're all friends, Sue.
We should get to work on our to-do list.
Sue's right.

We left to fly back to school while the Recycle Club stayed to collect more trash.

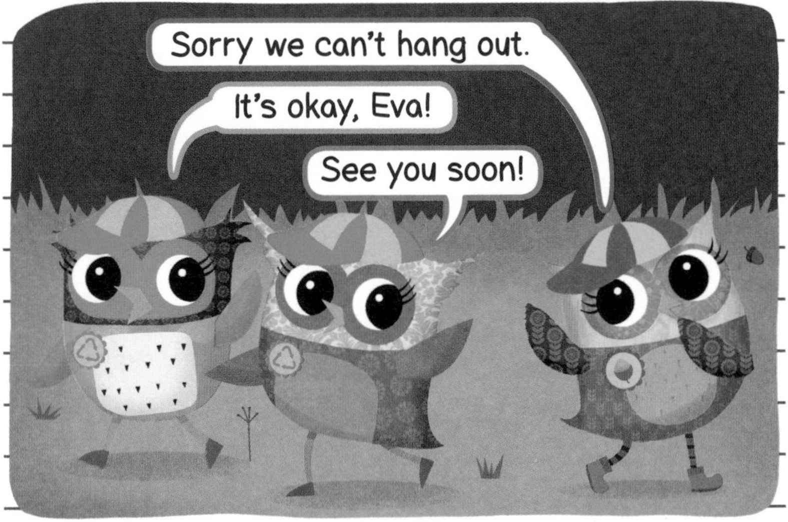
Sorry we can't hang out.
It's okay, Eva!
See you soon!

Back at school, we planted flower seeds in small pots. It was messy and fun!

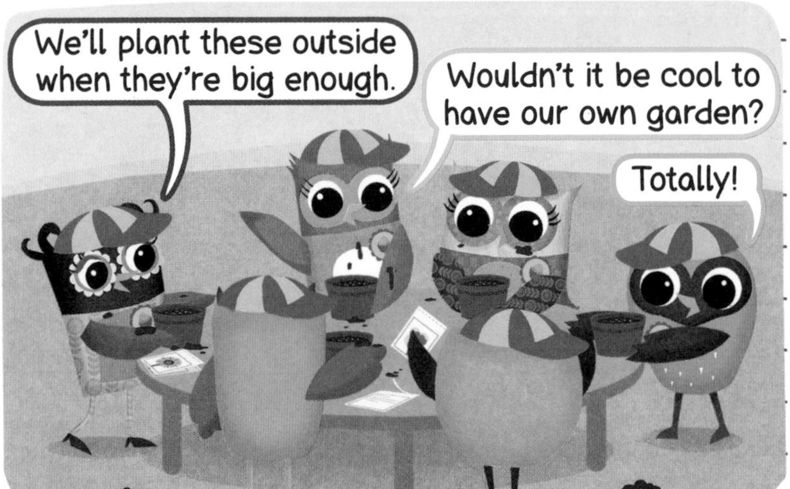
We'll plant these outside when they're big enough.
Wouldn't it be cool to have our own garden?
Totally!

Before we knew it, school was over.

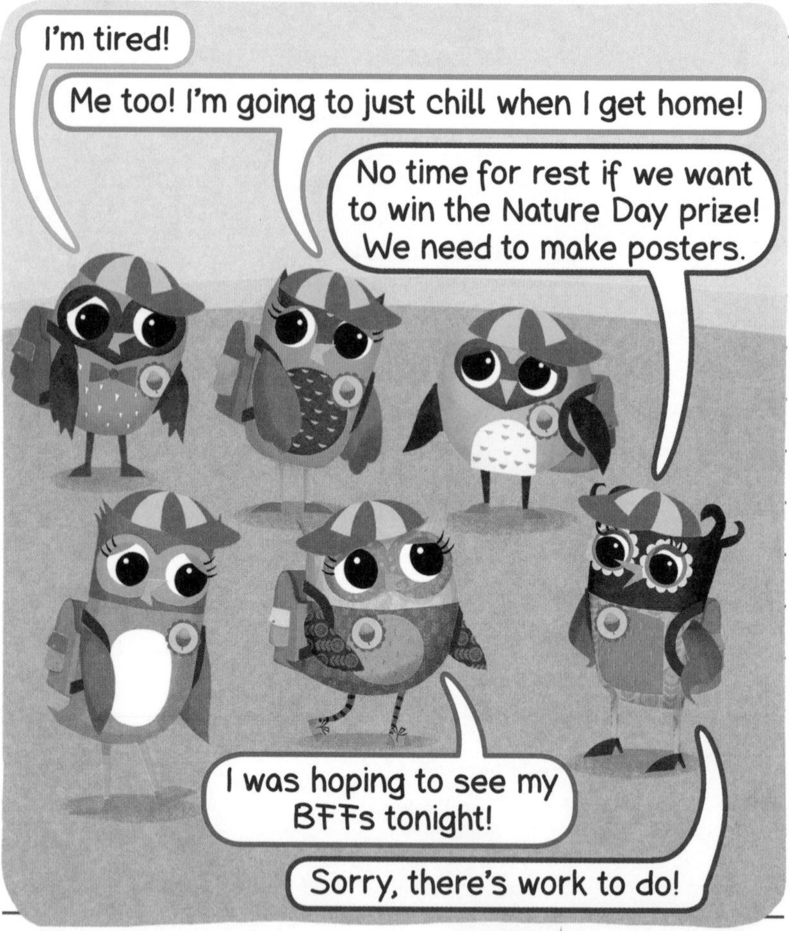

I'm tired!
Me too! I'm going to just chill when I get home!
No time for rest if we want to win the Nature Day prize! We need to make posters.
I was hoping to see my BFFs tonight!
Sorry, there's work to do!

I was making posters when Lucy and Hailey called.

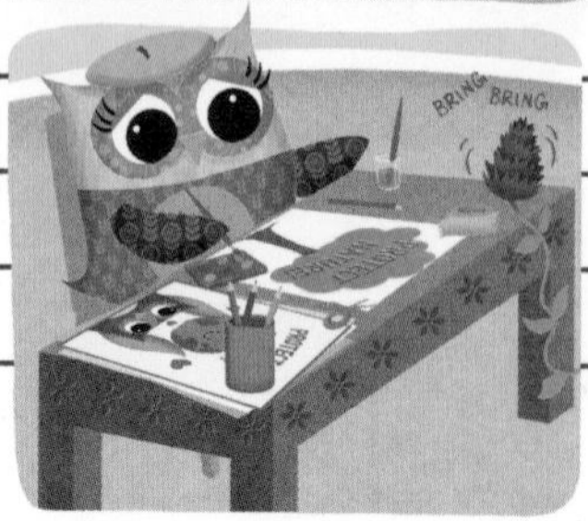

BRING
BRING

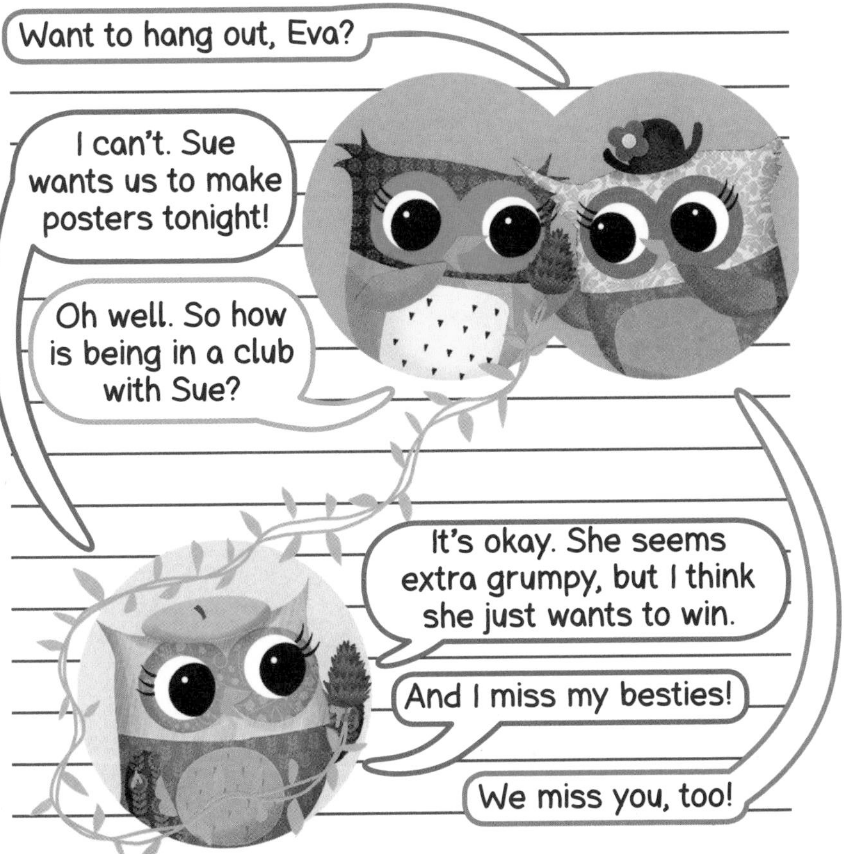
Want to hang out, Eva?
I can't. Sue wants us to make posters tonight!
Oh well. So how is being in a club with Sue?
It's okay. She seems extra grumpy, but I think she just wants to win.
And I miss my besties!
We miss you, too!

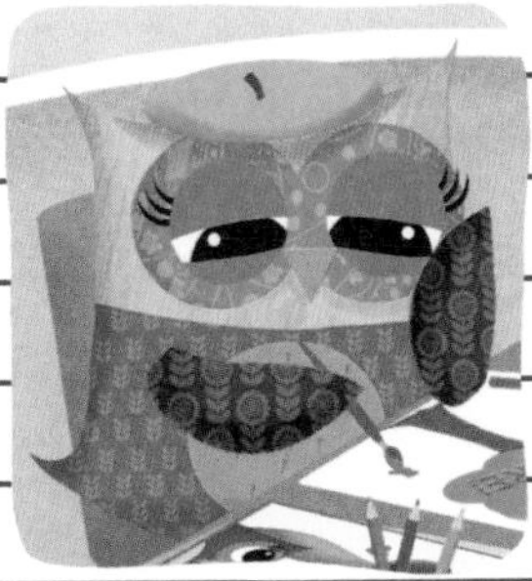

I miss hanging out with Lucy and Hailey. But I must finish these posters because I do want to win that prize (and save the planet, of course!).

♥ HOO Will Win? ♥

Wednesday

Tonight, the Nature Club designed and built our bug hotel.

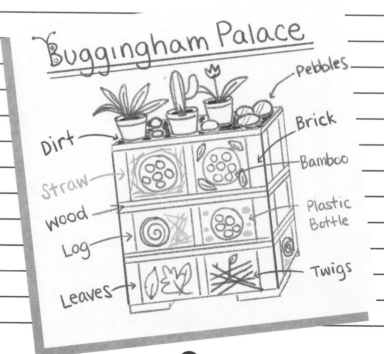

Buggingham Palace

Pebbles

Dirt

Brick

Straw

Bamboo

Wood

Plastic Bottle

Log

Leaves

Twigs

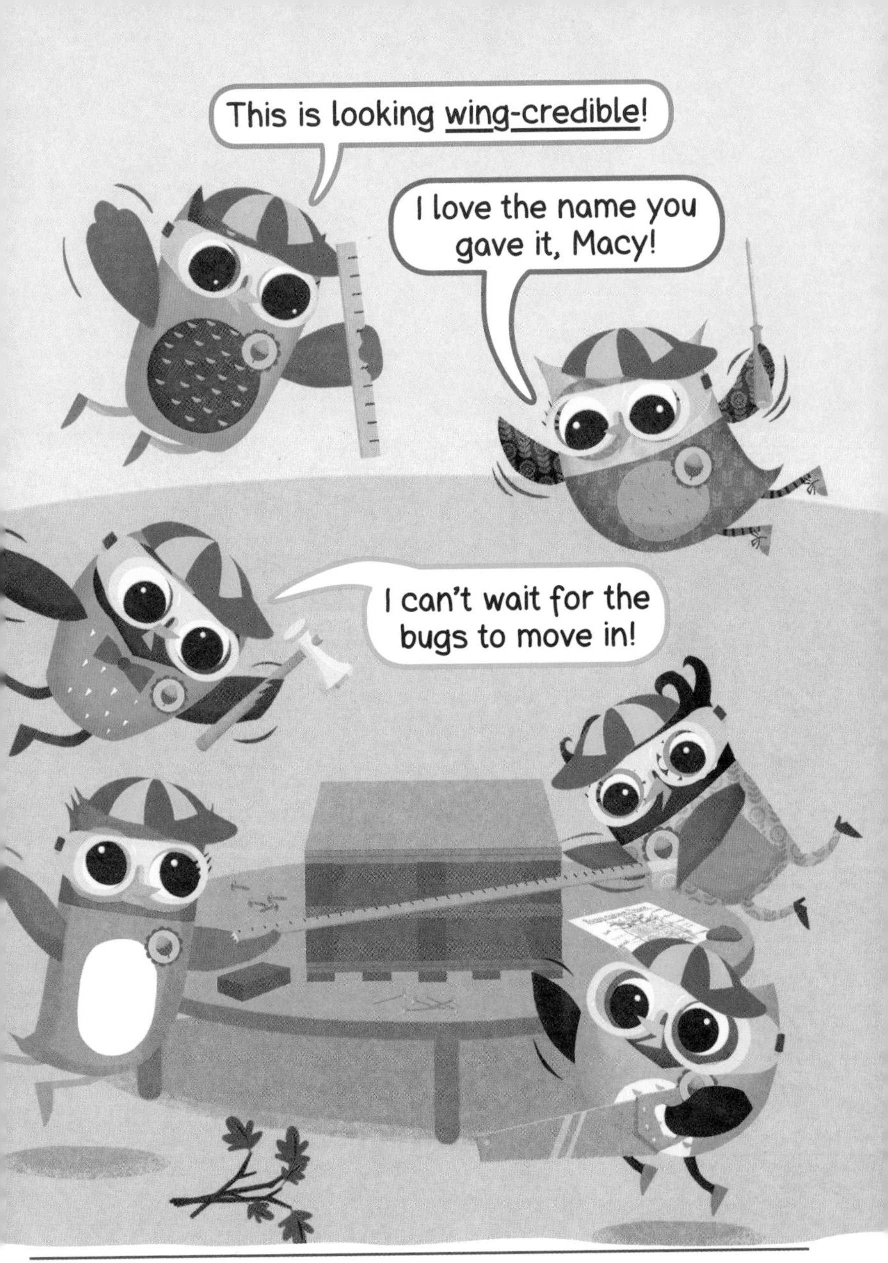
This is looking wing-credible!
I love the name you gave it, Macy!
I can't wait for the bugs to move in!

What do you think, Diary?

Mrs. Featherbottom stopped by to check on our project.

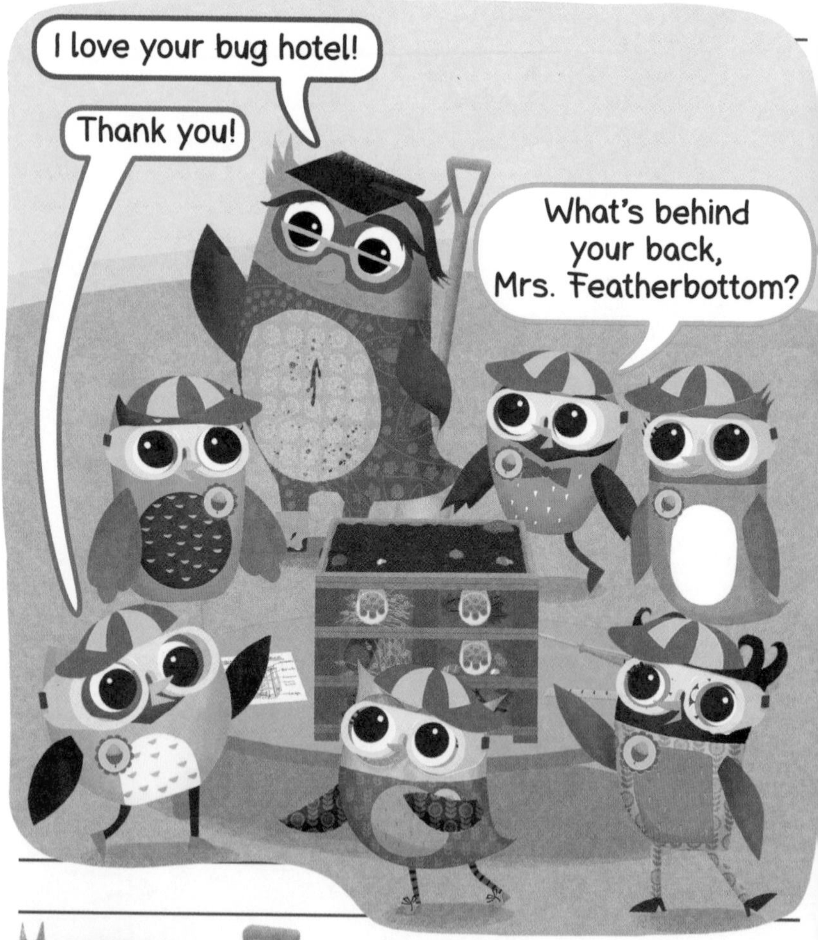
I love your bug hotel!
Thank you!
What's behind your back, Mrs. Featherbottom?

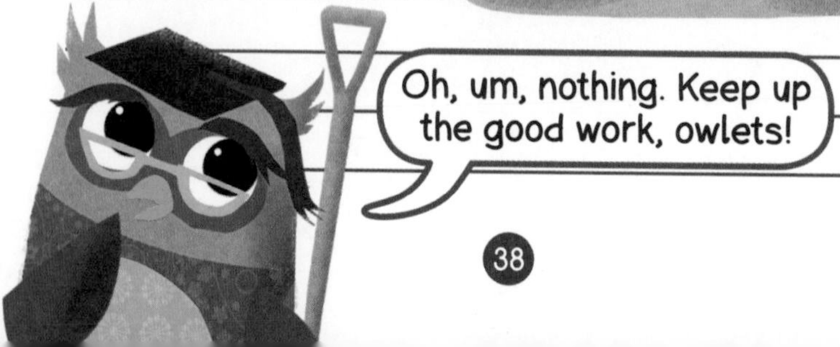
Oh, um, nothing. Keep up the good work, owlets!

Mrs. Featherbottom flapped away.

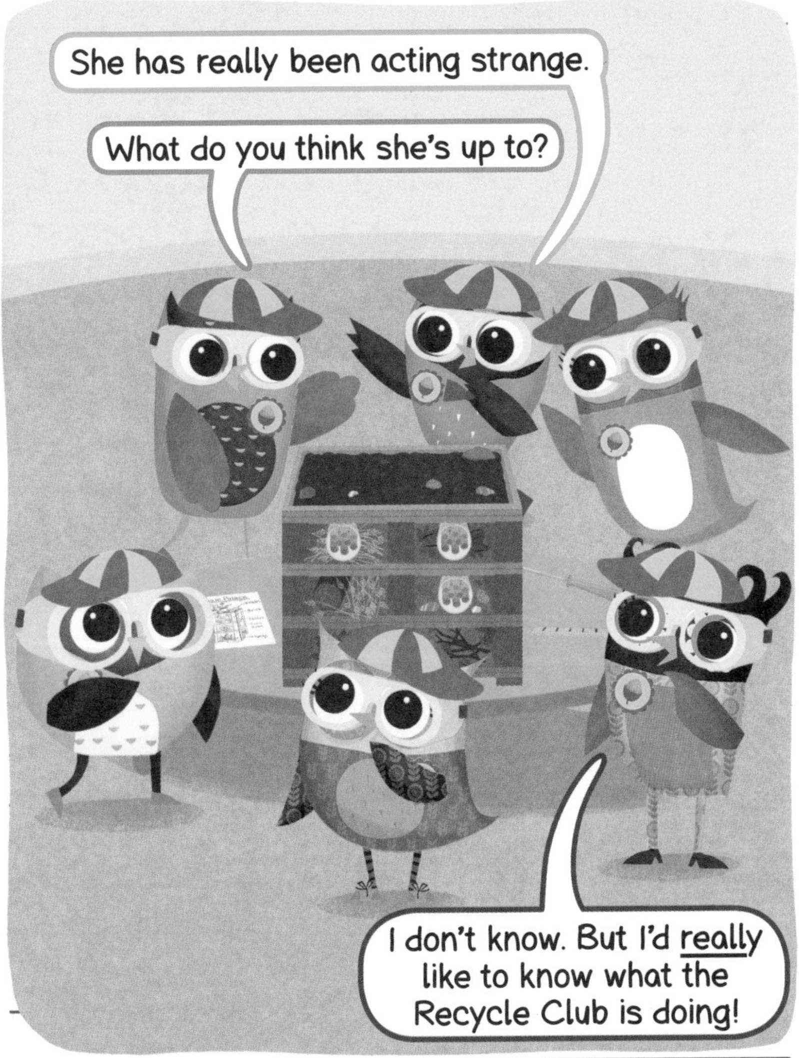

What do you think she's up to?
She has really been acting strange.
I don't know. But I'd really like to know what the Recycle Club is doing!

Just then, Lucy and Zara flew past . . .

Lucy was wearing a **BEHOOTIFUL** dress made from trash — like cardboard and plastic bottles. It wasn't finished, but it looked really cool!

I'll sew the top of the dress and it will fit great!

Thanks, Zara!

I thought Sue might be jealous that the other club was making clothes, since fashion is <u>her</u> passion. But she was being super nice to Zara!

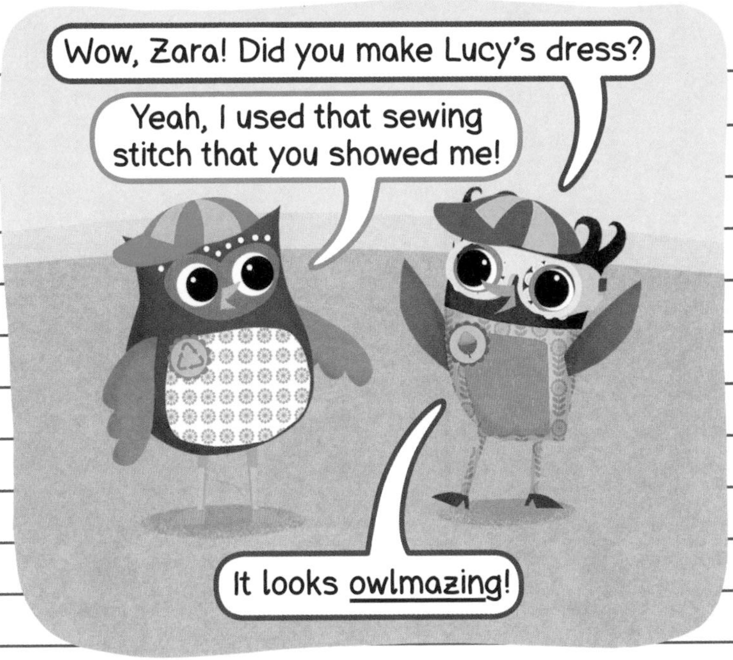
Wow, Zara! Did you make Lucy's dress?
Yeah, I used that sewing stitch that you showed me!
It looks owlmazing!

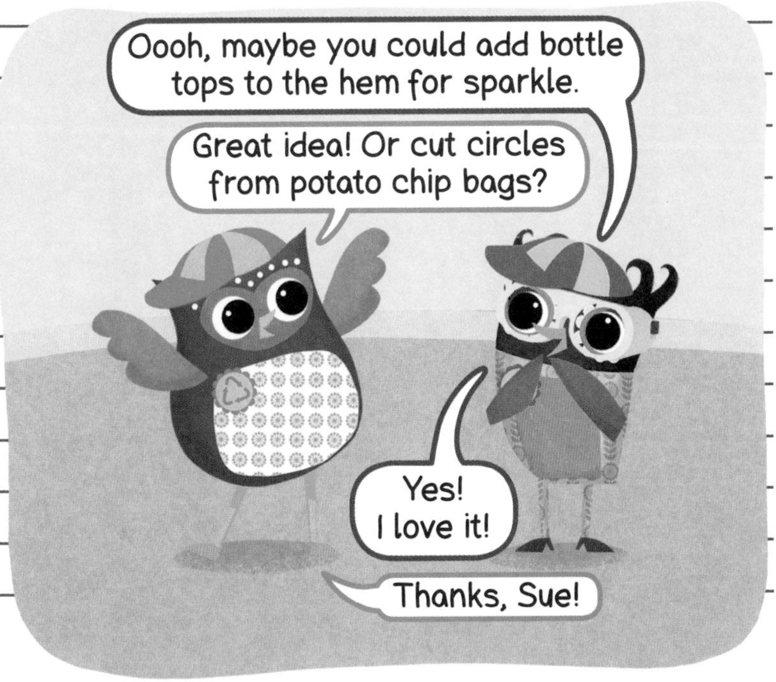
Oooh, maybe you could add bottle tops to the hem for sparkle.
Great idea! Or cut circles from potato chip bags?
Yes! I love it!
Thanks, Sue!

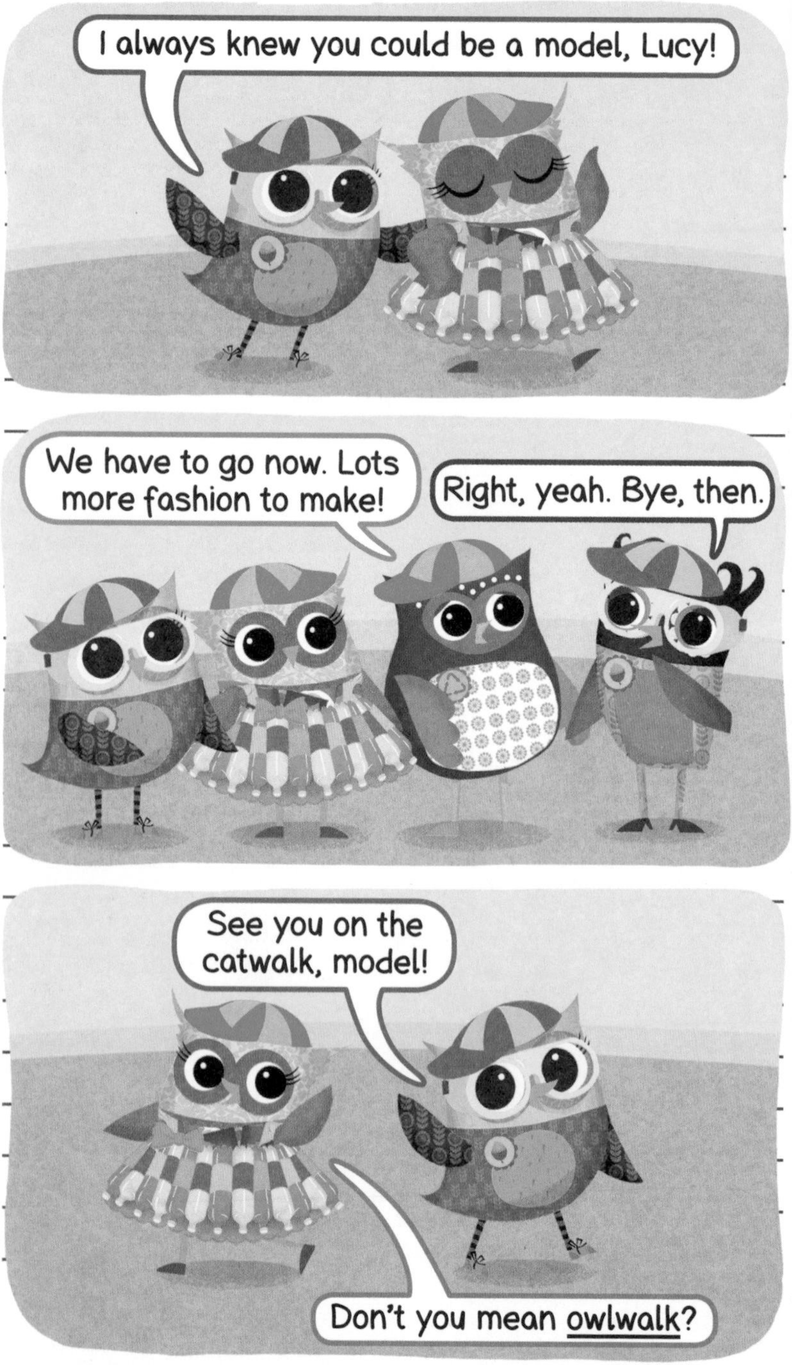
I always knew you could be a model, Lucy!
We have to go now. Lots more fashion to make!
Right, yeah. Bye, then.
See you on the catwalk, model!
Don't you mean owlwalk?

That recycled outfit looked wing-credible. Our club is never going to beat that!
All we have are some boring posters, and seeds no one can see.
And the bug hotel!
Yeah, I guess so.
We don't stand a chance of winning!

We needed to stop worrying that our club wasn't as good as the Recycle Club.

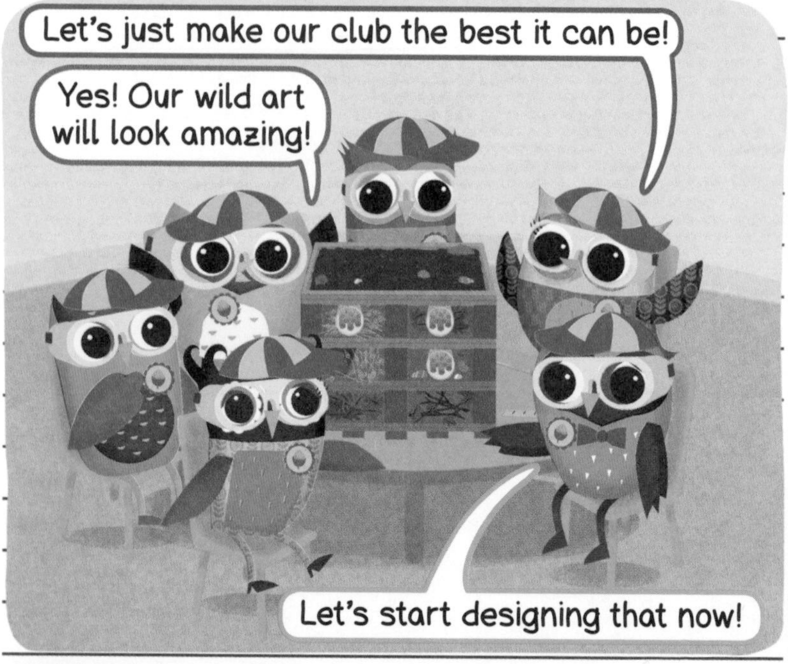
Let's just make our club the best it can be!
Yes! Our wild art will look amazing!
Let's start designing that now!

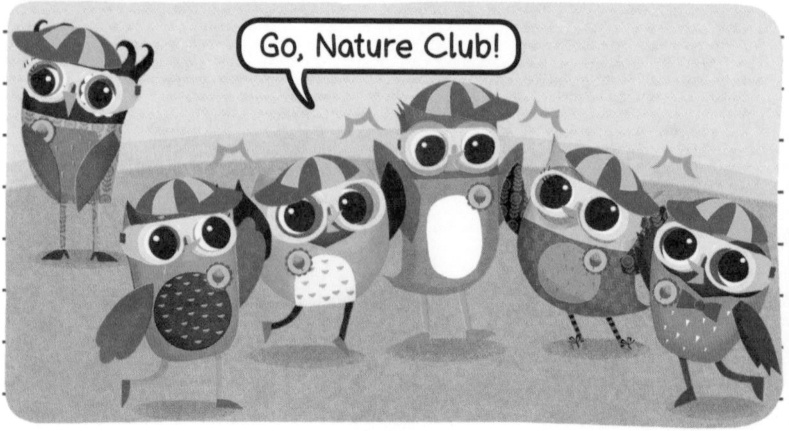
Go, Nature Club!

As we designed our wild art, I saw that Sue looked upset.

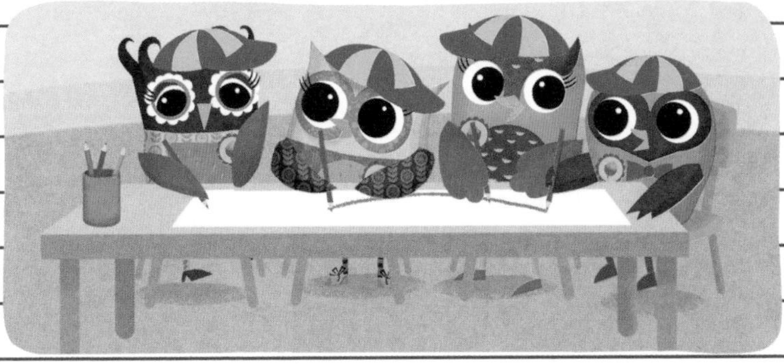

Before we flew off to hang our posters, I asked if she was okay.

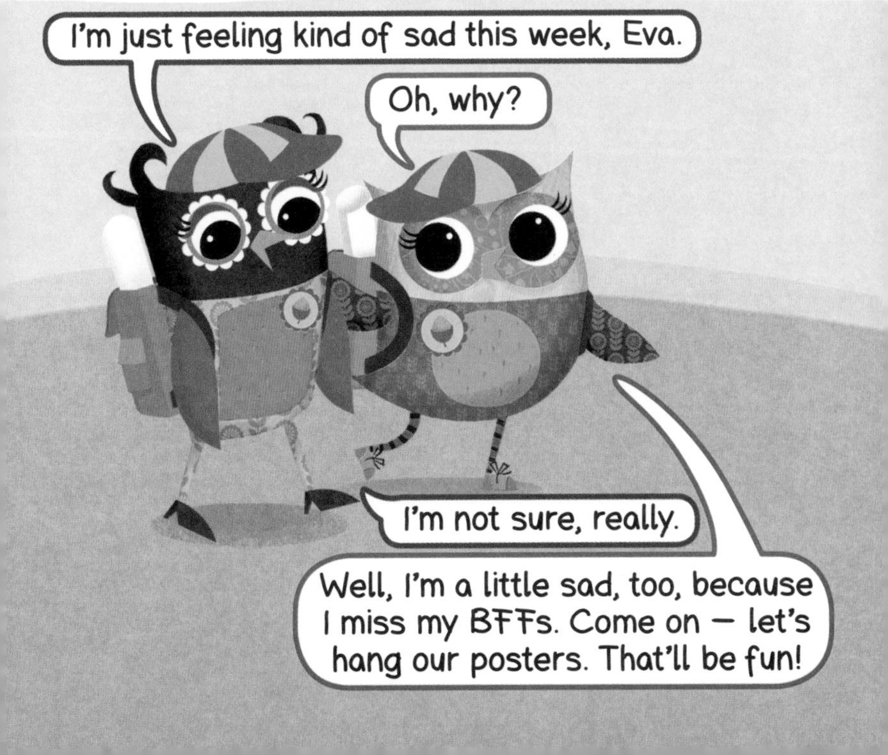
I'm just feeling kind of sad this week, Eva.
Oh, why?
I'm not sure, really.
Well, I'm a little sad, too, because I miss my BFFs. Come on — let's hang our posters. That'll be fun!

While we hung our posters around the forest, Jacob and Macy kept making me laugh.

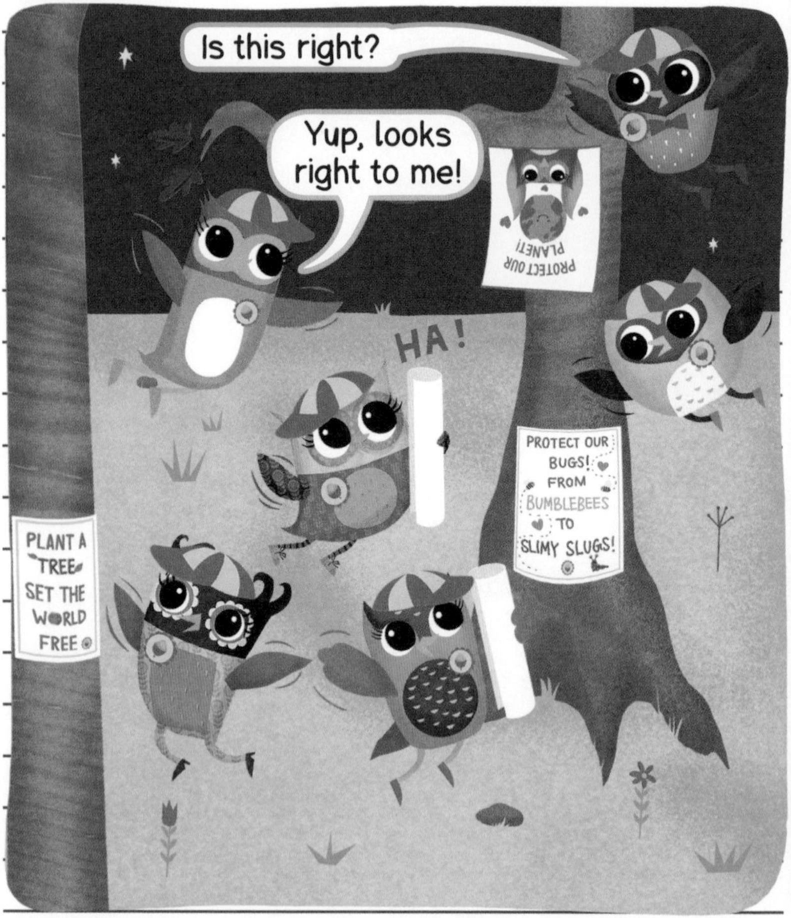
Is this right?
Yup, looks right to me!
PROTECT OUR PLANET!
HA!
PROTECT OUR BUGS! FROM BUMBLEBEES TO SLIMY SLUGS!
PLANT A TREE SET THE WORLD FREE

They're so funny! How did I not know that about them?

The Recycle Club was putting up their posters, too.

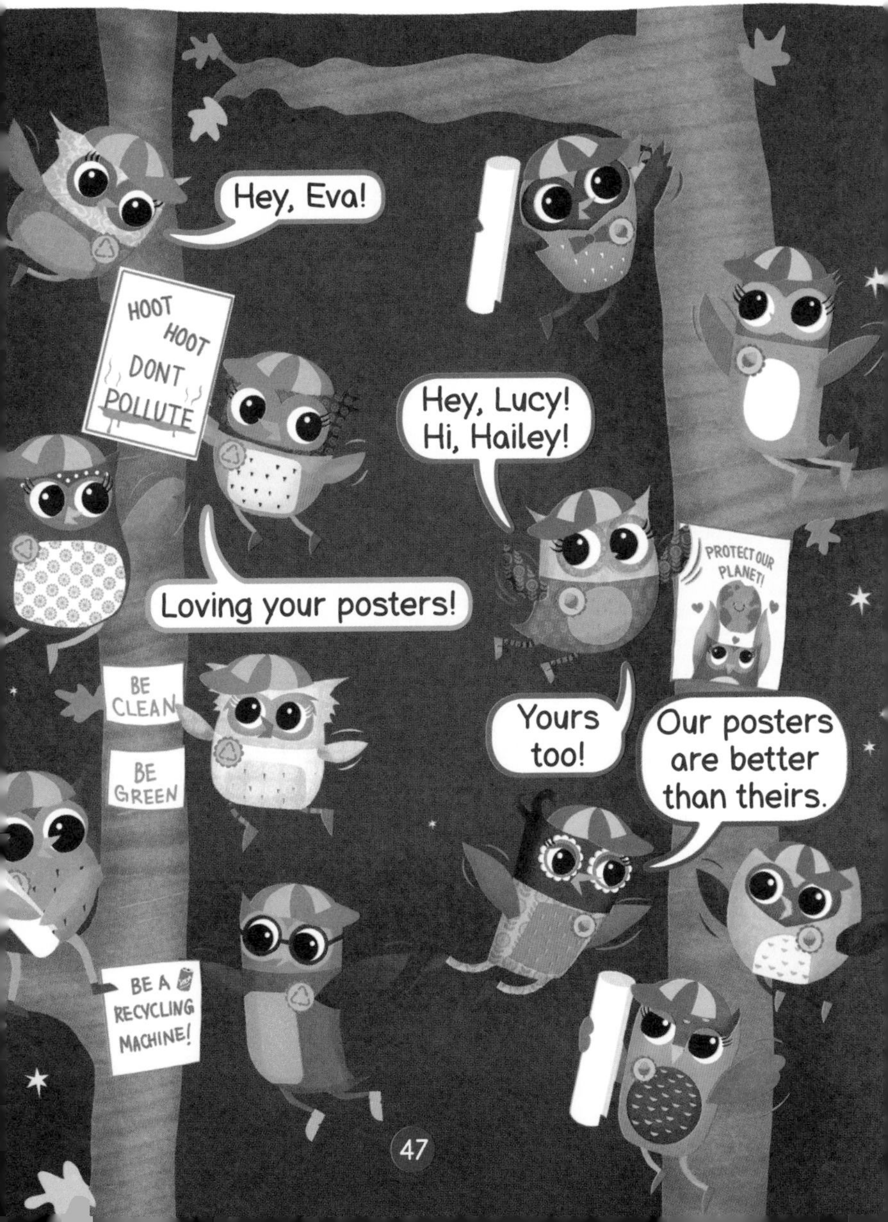
Hey, Eva!
HOOT HOOT DONT POLLUTE
Hey, Lucy! Hi, Hailey!
Loving your posters!
PROTECT OUR PLANET!
BE CLEAN
BE GREEN
Yours too!
Our posters are better than theirs.
BE A RECYCLING MACHINE!

Diary, Sue is feeling sad and I think it's making her act mean. I wish I could figure out <u>why</u> she's unhappy . . .

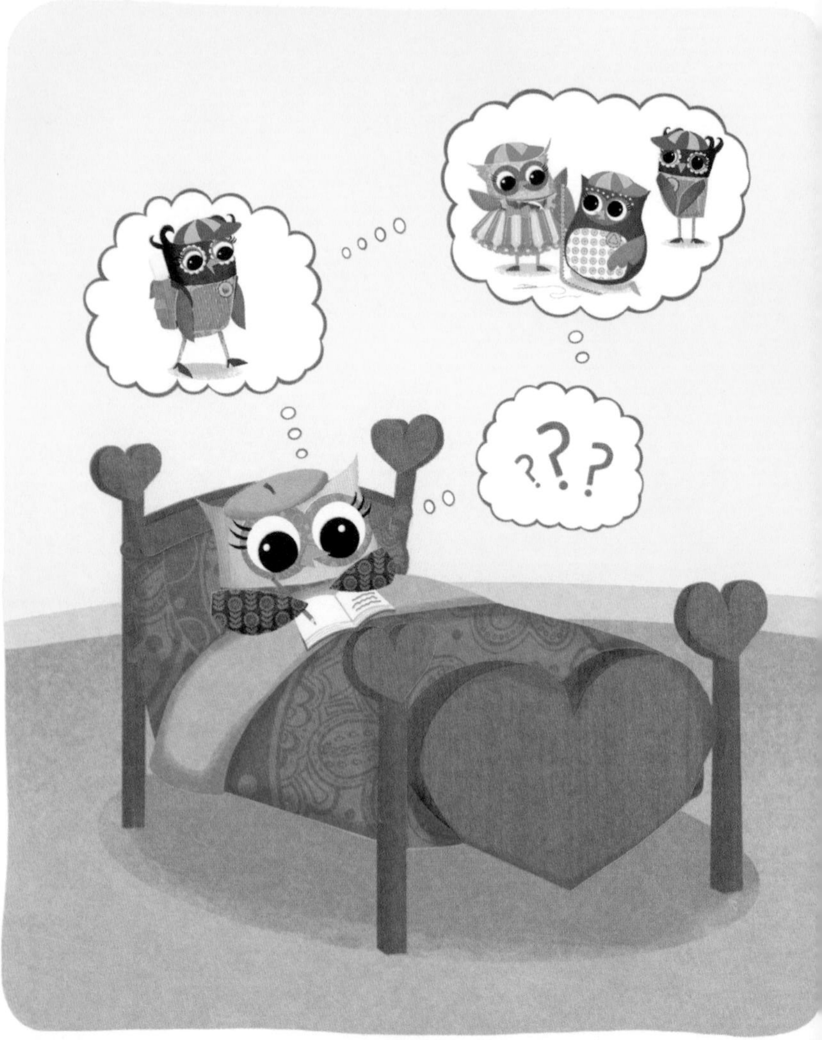
???

5

♡ Best Feathery Friends Forever ♡

Thursday

Mrs. Featherbottom kept yawning while teaching tonight.

Are you okay, Mrs. Featherbottom?
Oh! Yes. Just tired, Jacob!

After lunch, we collected more materials for our **FLAPPY-FABULOUS** wild art. Then we started making it.

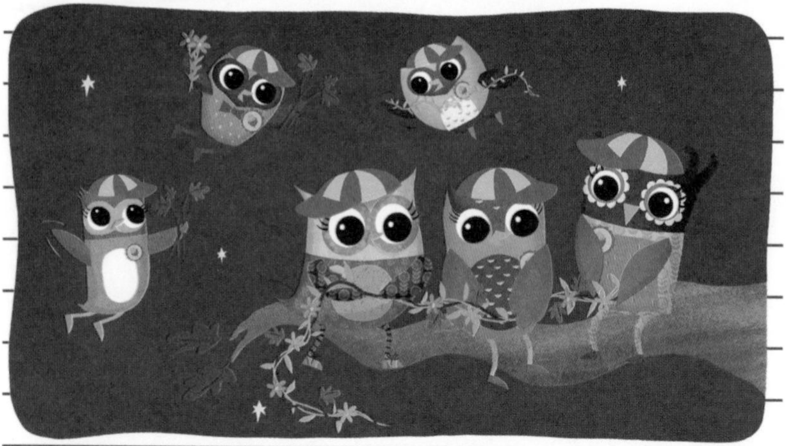

We also played around!

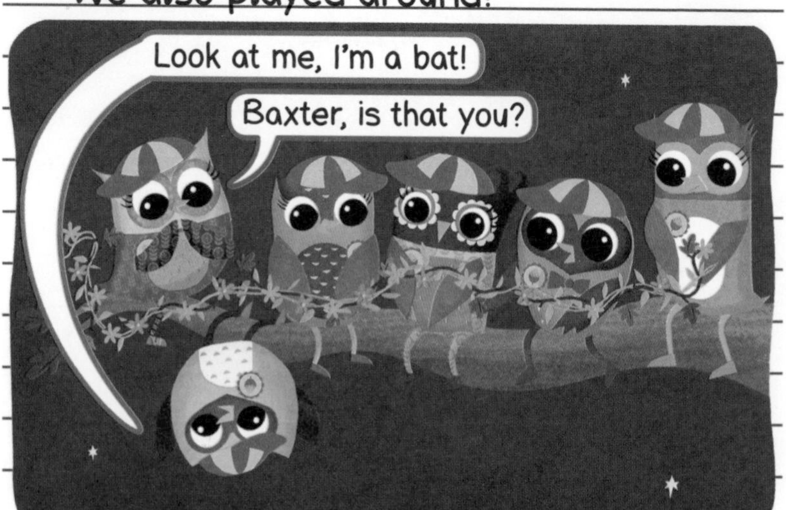
Look at me, I'm a bat!
Baxter, is that you?

I realized that I've gotten to know these friends so much better being in our club this week. They're really kind and funny!

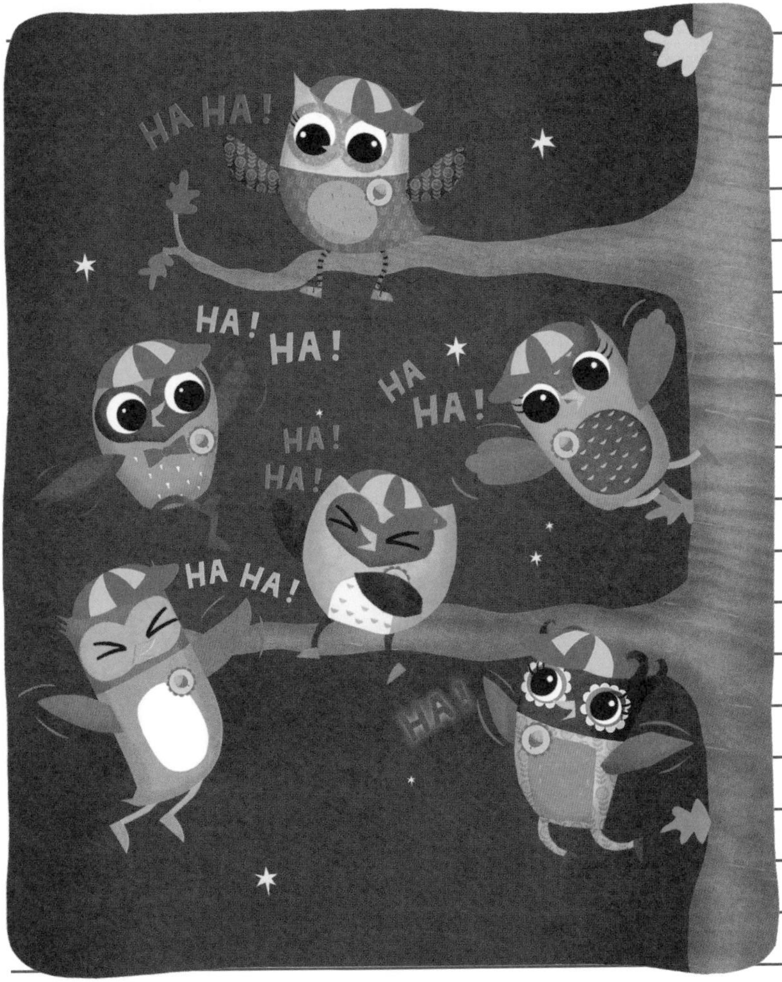
HA HA!
HA!
HA!
HA HA!
HA!
HA!
HA HA!
HA!

Back at home, I thought of how I still missed Lucy and Hailey. But I hoped they were having fun with their club mates, just like I was!

Then the doorbell rang.

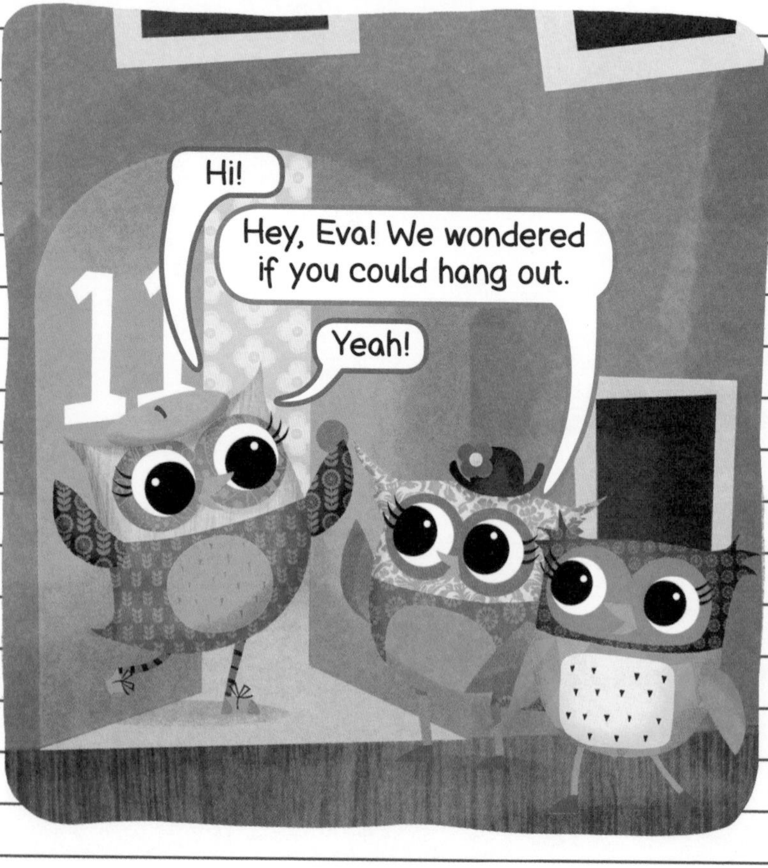
Hi!
Hey, Eva! We wondered if you could hang out.
Yeah!

We had the most fun ever!

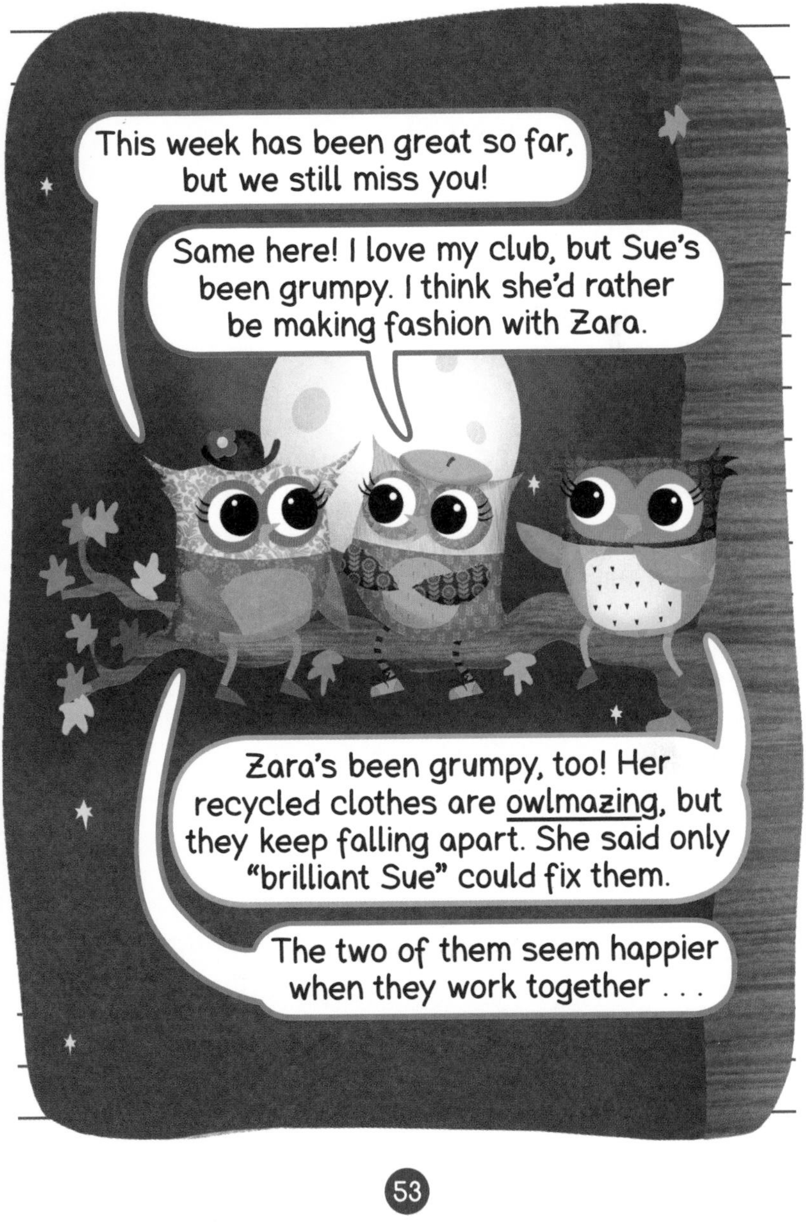
This week has been great so far, but we still miss you!
Same here! I love my club, but Sue's been grumpy. I think she'd rather be making fashion with Zara.
Zara's been grumpy, too! Her recycled clothes are owlmazing, but they keep falling apart. She said only "brilliant Sue" could fix them.
The two of them seem happier when they work together . . .

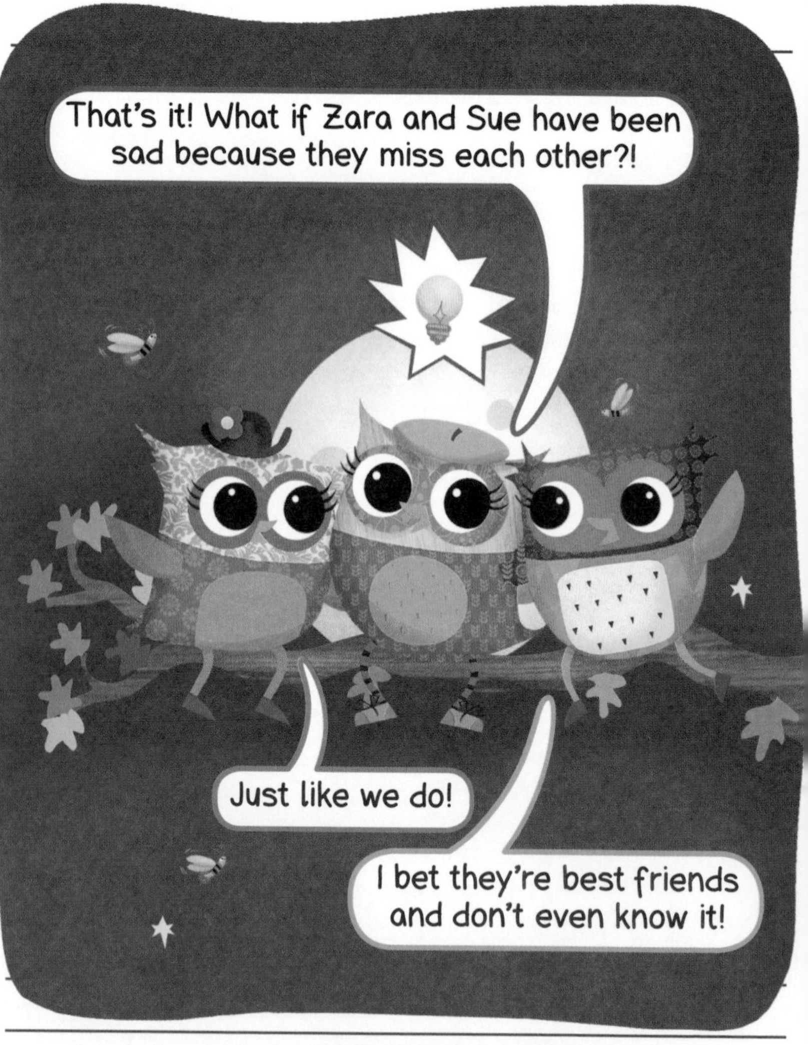
That's it! What if Zara and Sue have been sad because they miss each other?!
Just like we do!
I bet they're best friends and don't even know it!

I had such a **HOOTIFUL** time with my besties. How can we help Zara and Sue realize that they're best friends, too? Oh, Diary – I have an idea!

6

Together Again

Friday

At school, Mrs. Featherbottom was trying to hide something behind her back.

Class, I have to pop out for a minute.
Keep working on your presentations!

The Nature Club watered our seeds and finished our wild art.

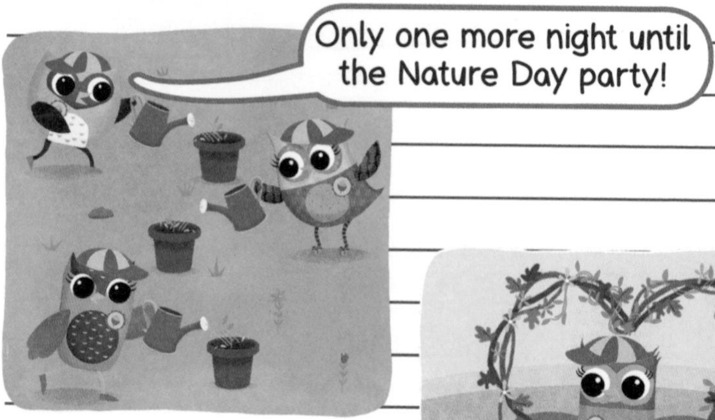
Only one more night until the Nature Day party!

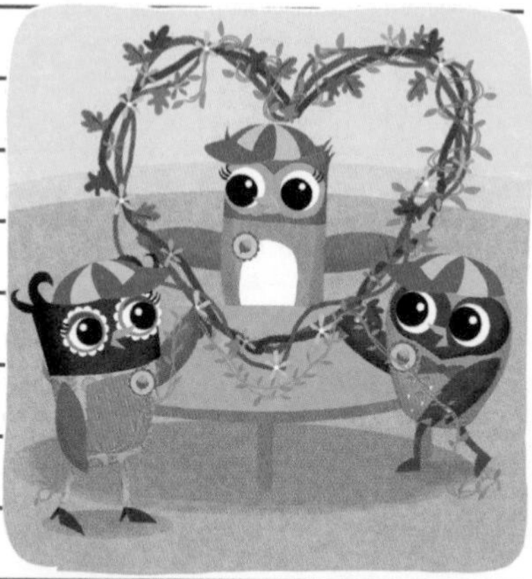

We brought everything to the Old Oak Tree to set up for tomorrow.

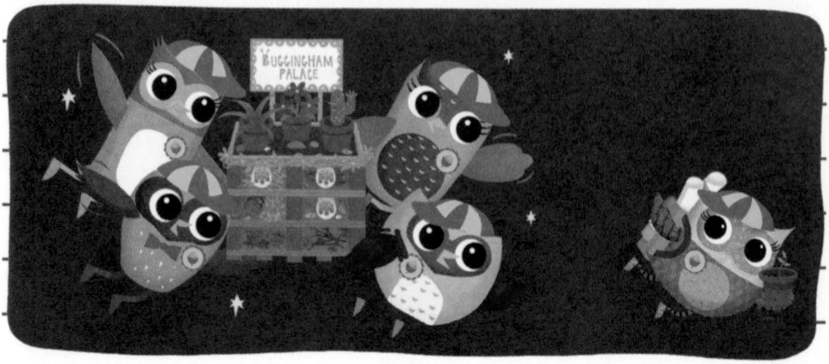
BUGGINGHAM PALACE

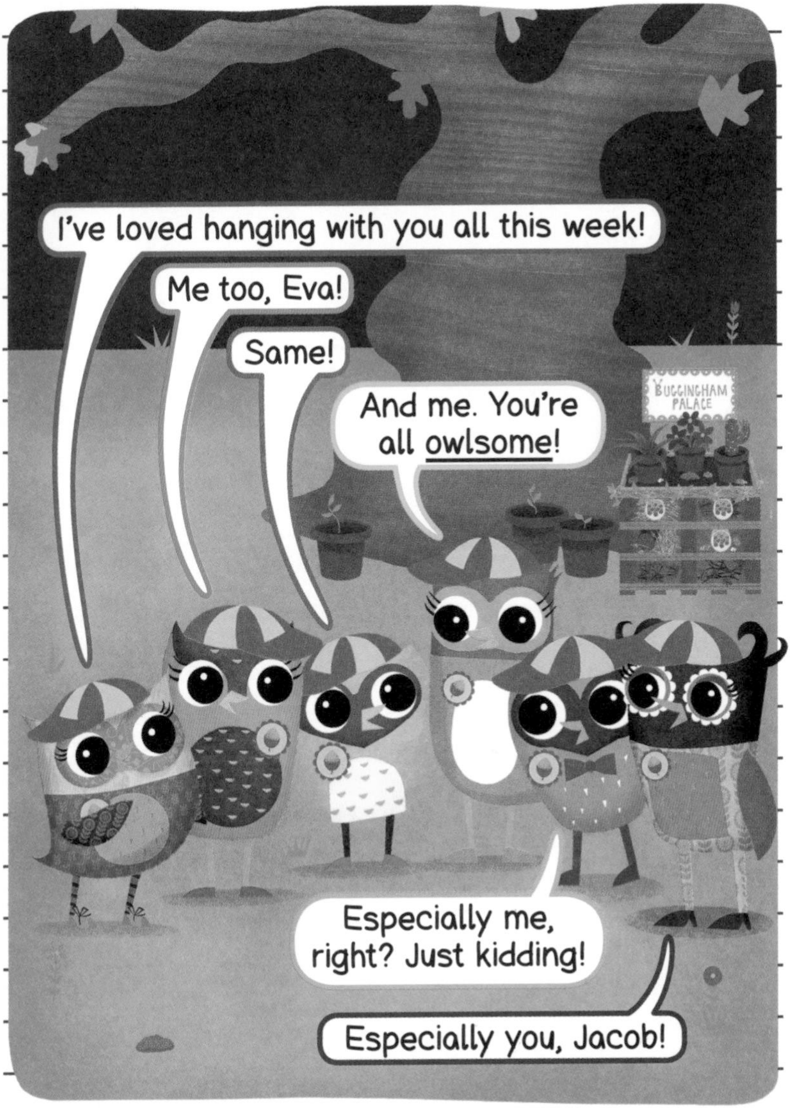
I've loved hanging with you all this week!
Me too, Eva!
Same!
And me. You're all owlsome!
BUGGINGHAM PALACE
Especially me, right? Just kidding!
Especially you, Jacob!

While everyone was working, I pulled Sue aside. Time to put my idea into action!

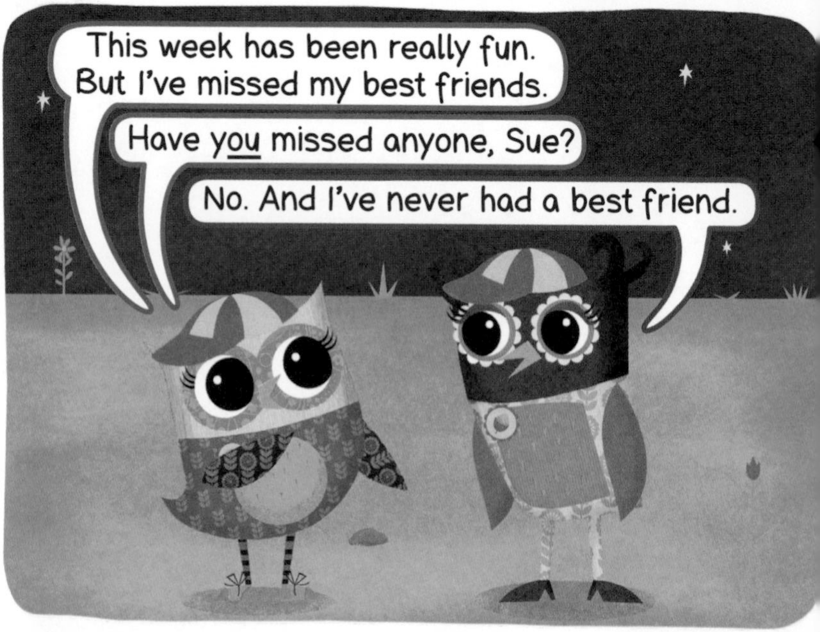
This week has been really fun. But I've missed my best friends.
Have you missed anyone, Sue?
No. And I've never had a best friend.

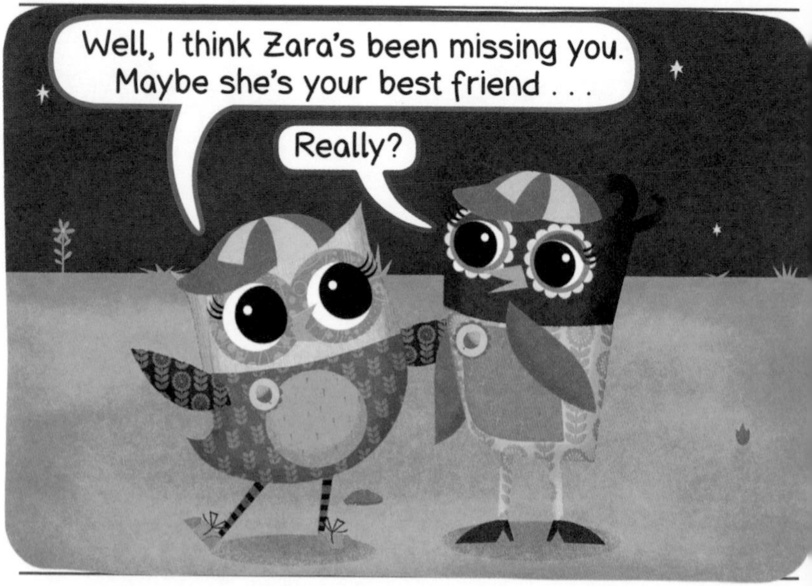
Well, I think Zara's been missing you. Maybe she's your best friend . . .
Really?

Then the Recycle Club arrived.

I went over to Zara.

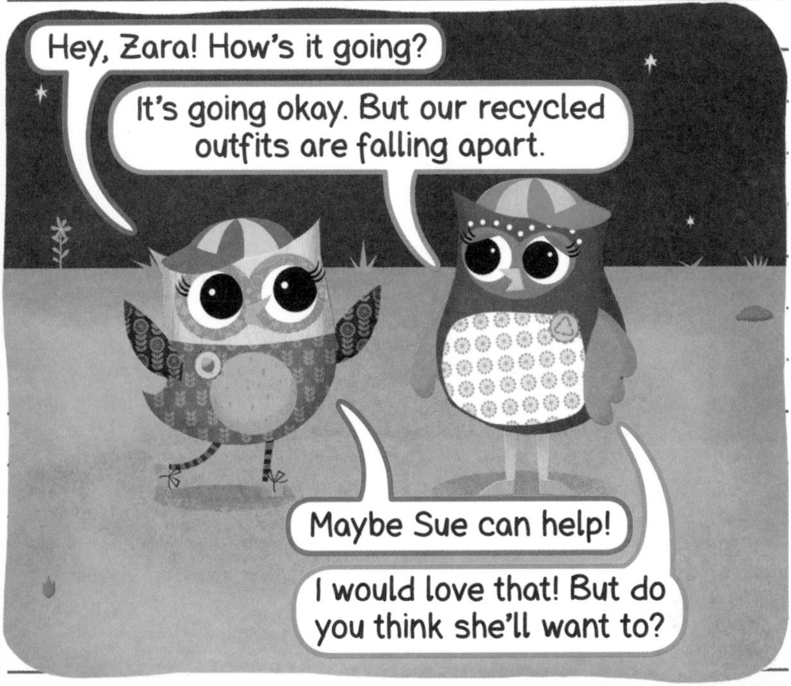
Hey, Zara! How's it going?
It's going okay. But our recycled outfits are falling apart.
Maybe Sue can help!
I would love that! But do you think she'll want to?

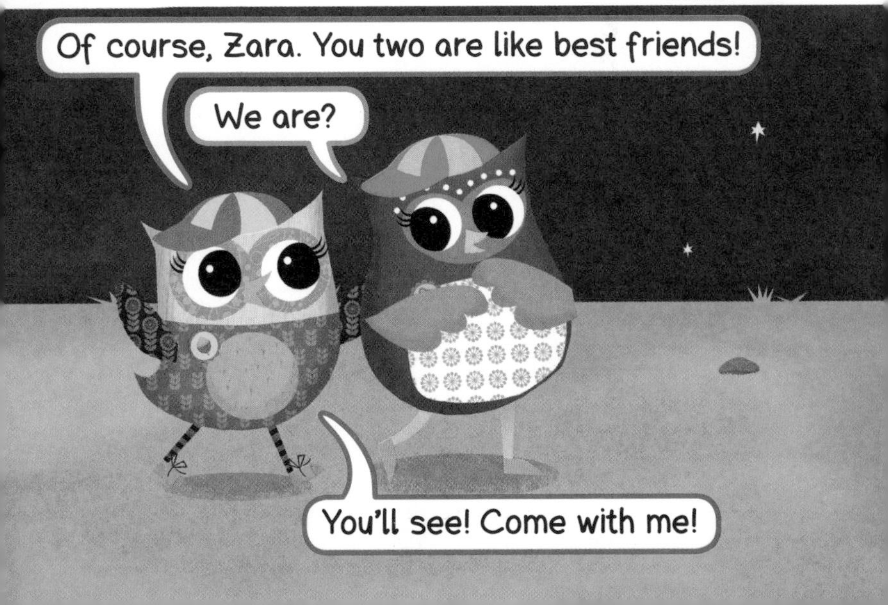
Of course, Zara. You two are like best friends!
We are?
You'll see! Come with me!

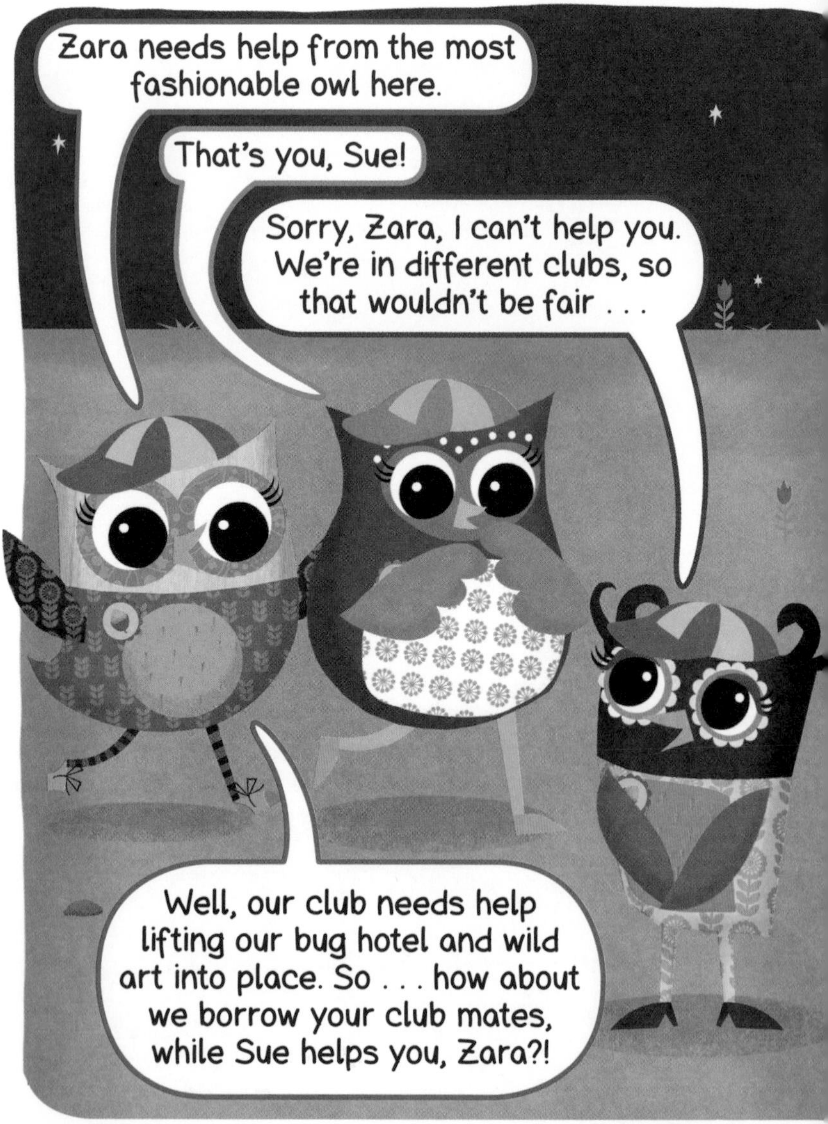
Zara needs help from the most fashionable owl here.
That's you, Sue!
Sorry, Zara, I can't help you. We're in different clubs, so that wouldn't be fair . . .
Well, our club needs help lifting our bug hotel and wild art into place. So . . . how about we borrow your club mates, while Sue helps you, Zara?!

Sue and Zara liked my suggestion!

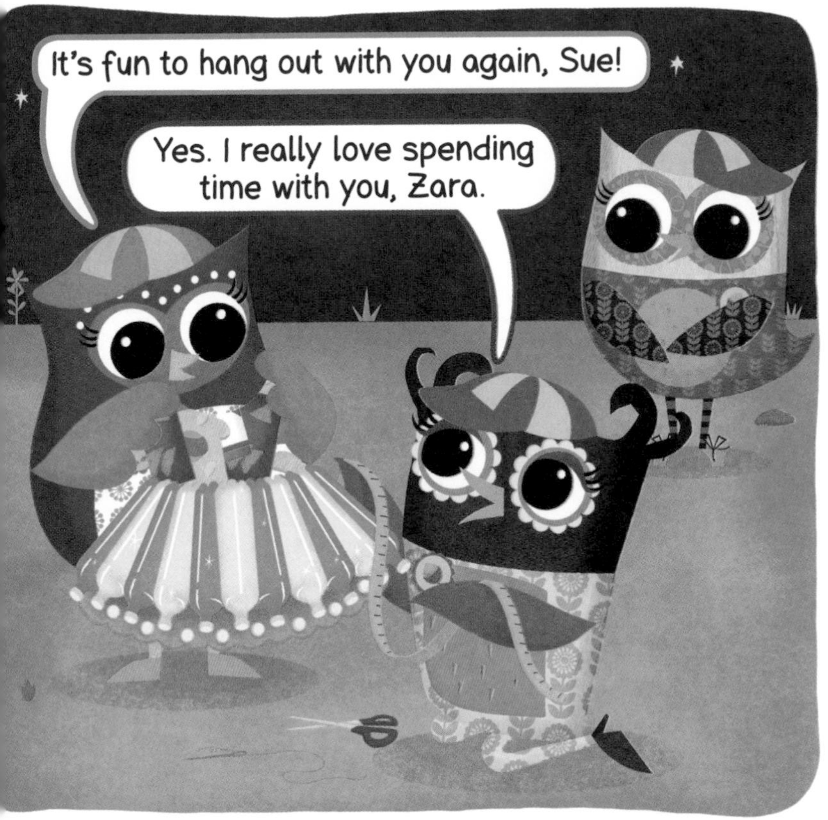
It's fun to hang out with you again, Sue!
Yes. I really love spending time with you, Zara.

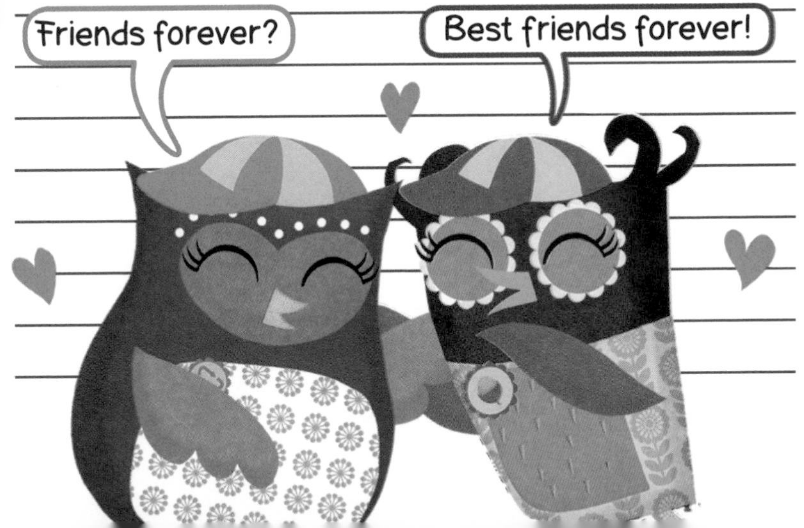
Friends forever?
Best friends forever!

Both clubs worked together to finish setting up for Nature Day.

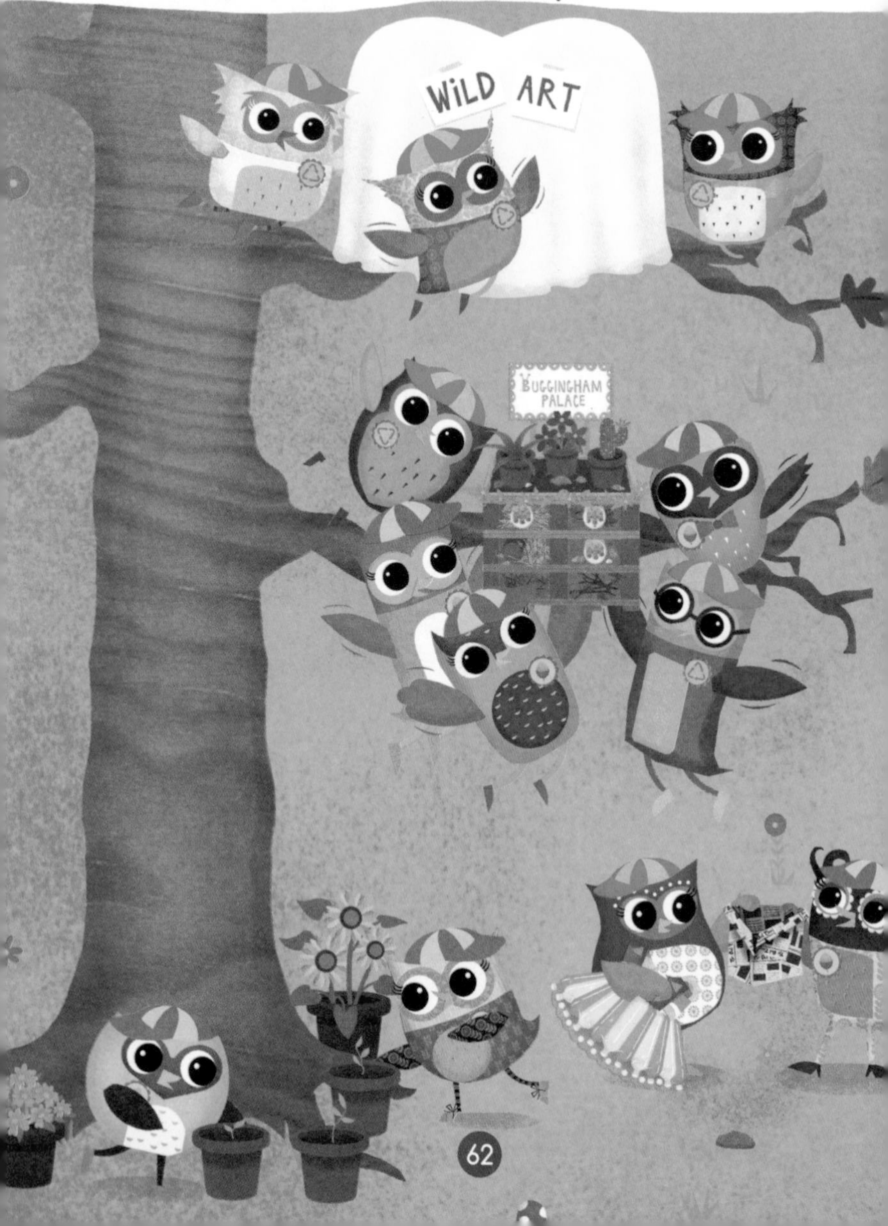
WILD ART
BUGGINGHAM PALACE

Then we all flew home.

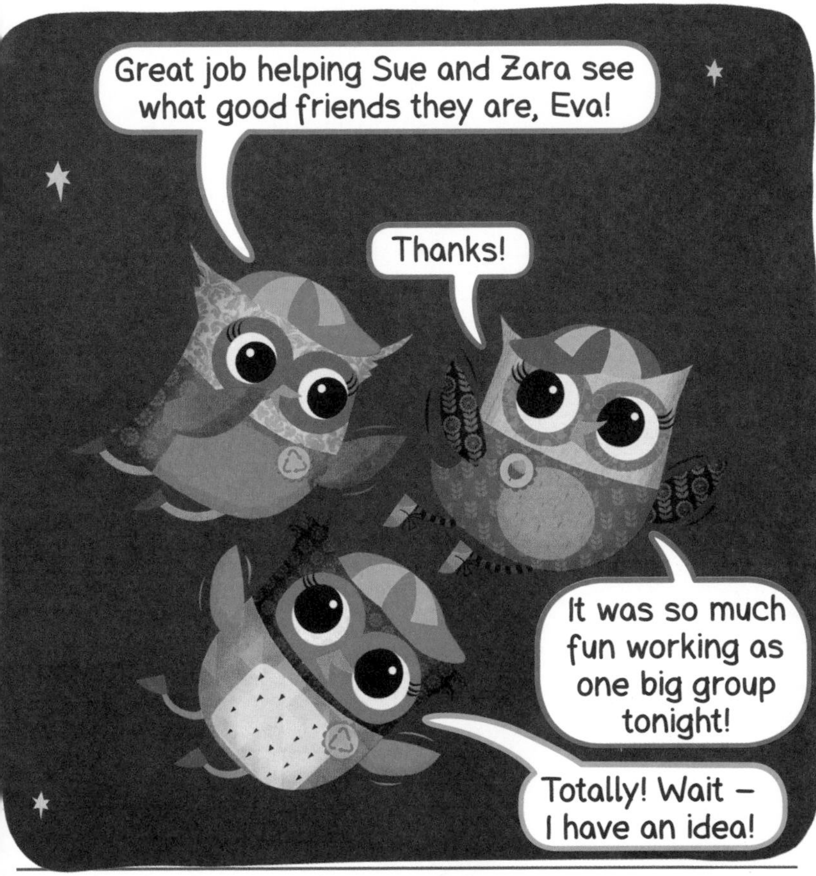
Great job helping Sue and Zara see what good friends they are, Eva!
Thanks!
It was so much fun working as one big group tonight!
Totally! Wait – I have an idea!

Diary, my besties and I made the best plan ever! But now I'm so tired . . .

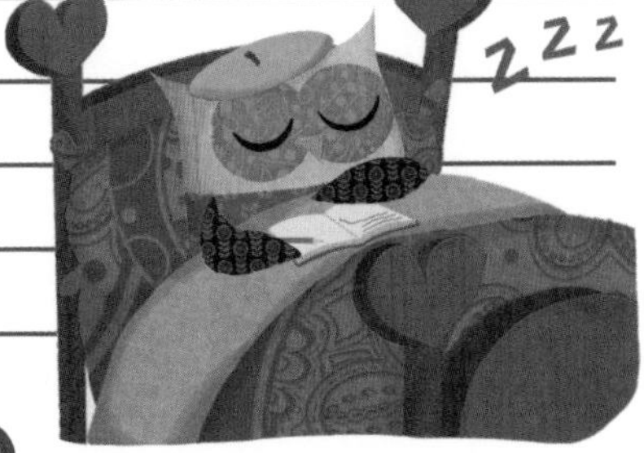
Z Z Z

7

♡ The Grand Prize ♡

Saturday

Nature Day finally arrived! Everyone in Treetopolis gathered at the Old Oak Tree to celebrate.

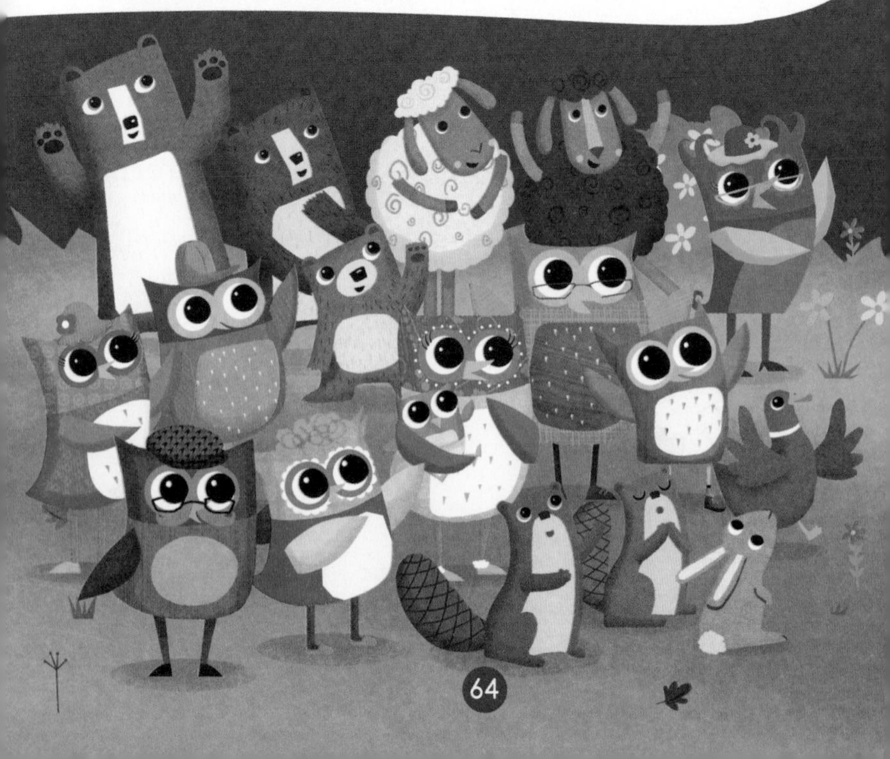

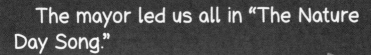

The mayor led us all in "The Nature Day Song."

Owls around the earth unite
To make our planet clean and bright.
The earth, it needs our love a lot
'Cause it's the only one we've got!

Soon, it was time for our presentations.

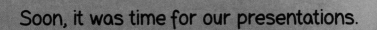

The Recycle Club showed everyone how to reuse and recycle.

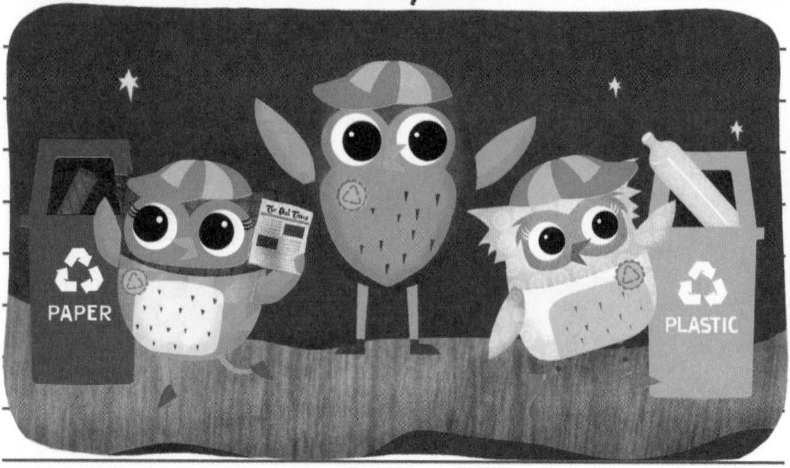
PAPER
PLASTIC

Then they put on a fashion show in their **FLAPPY-FABULOUS** outfits.

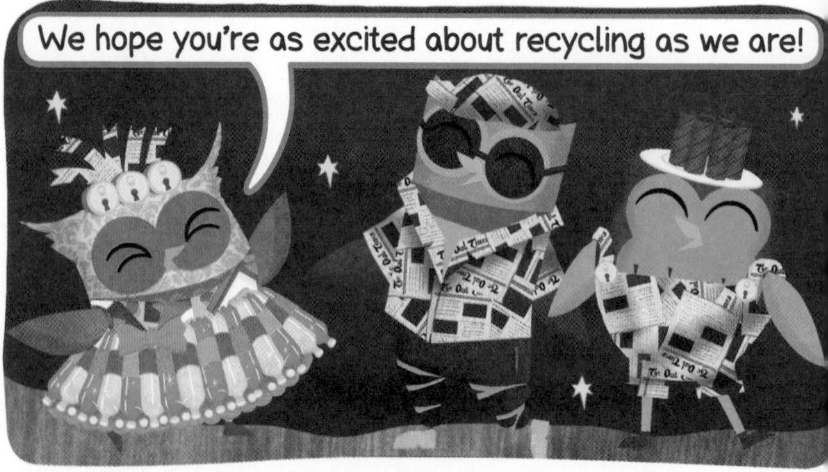
We hope you're as excited about recycling as we are!

Everyone clapped and cheered!

The Nature Club presented our bug hotel and our new seedlings.

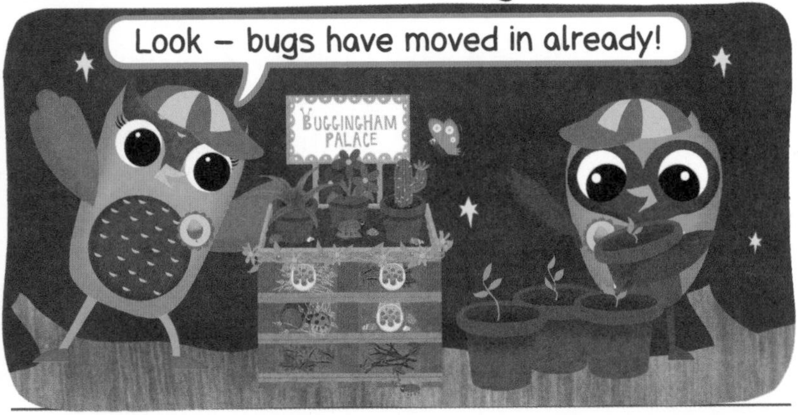
Look – bugs have moved in already!
BUGGINGHAM PALACE

Then we shared our wild art project!

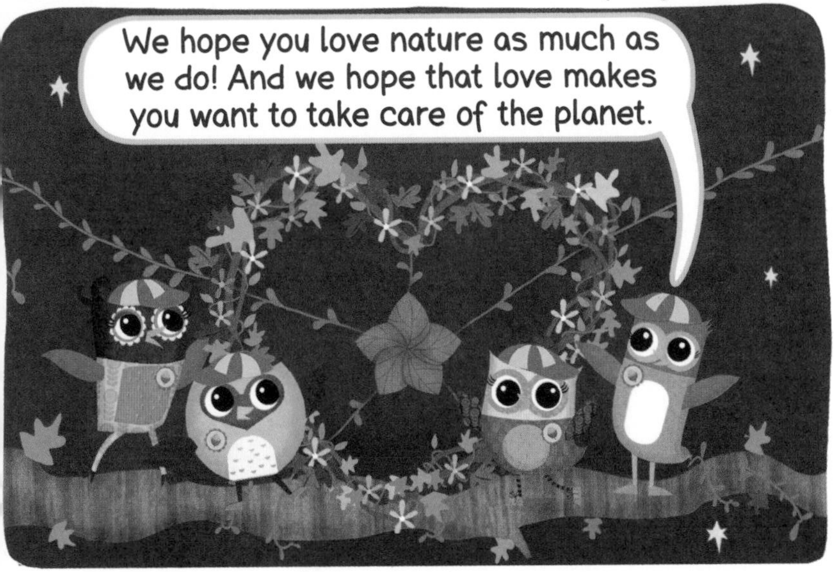
We hope you love nature as much as we do! And we hope that love makes you want to take care of the planet.

Everyone clapped and cheered again!

Mrs. Featherbottom stepped up to the microphone next.

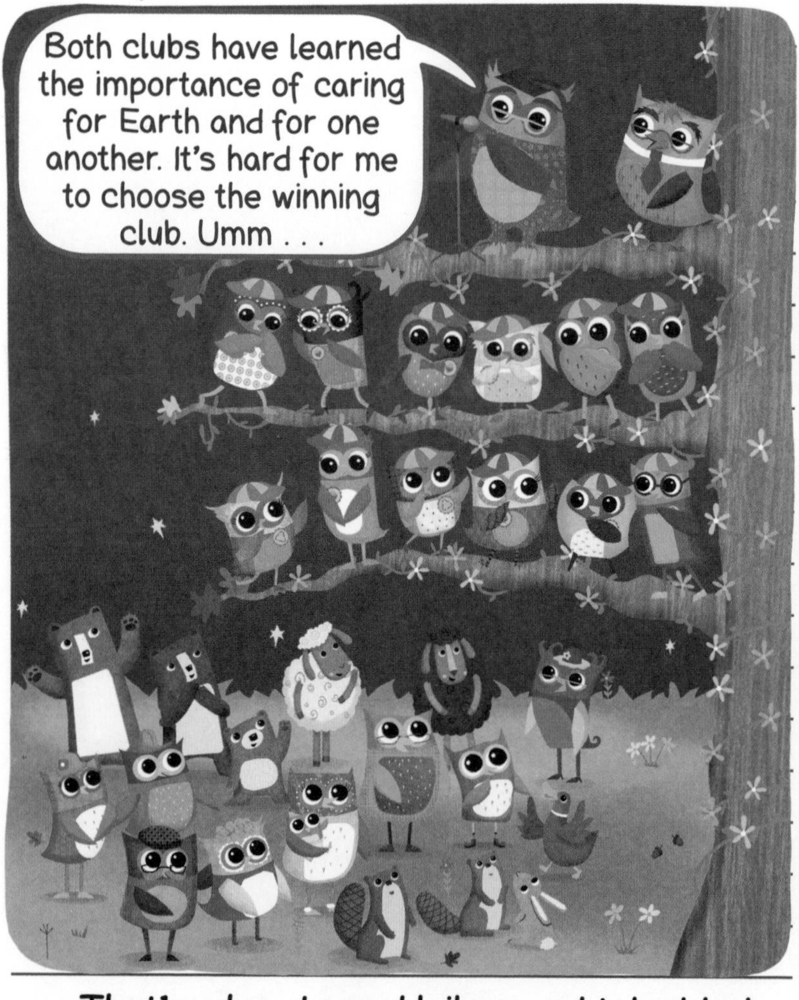
Both clubs have learned the importance of caring for Earth and for one another. It's hard for me to choose the winning club. Umm . . .

That's when Lucy, Hailey, and I decided to speak up.

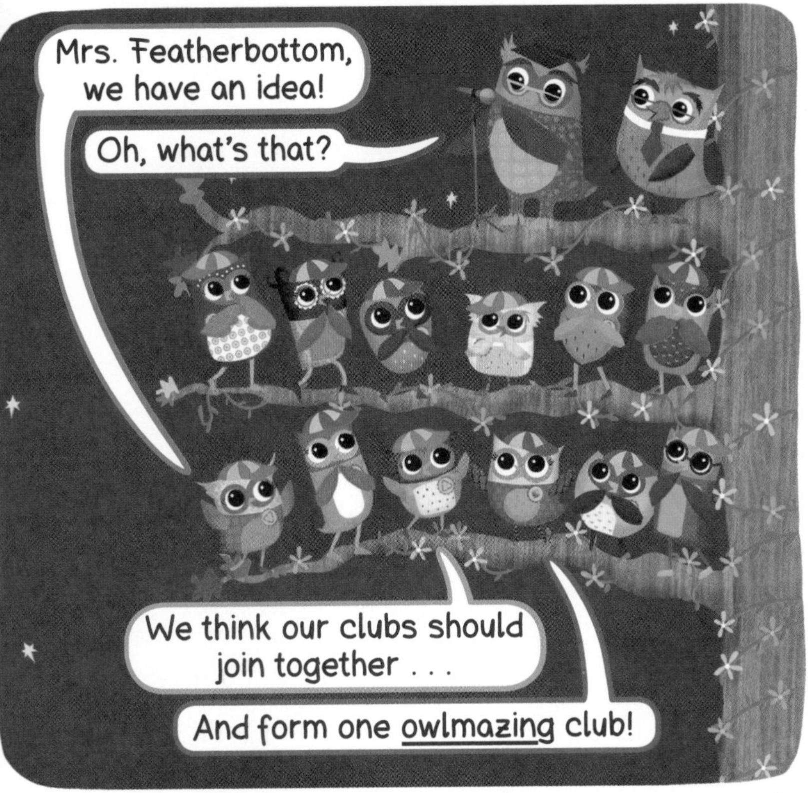
Mrs. Featherbottom, we have an idea!
Oh, what's that?
We think our clubs should join together . . .
And form one owlmazing club!

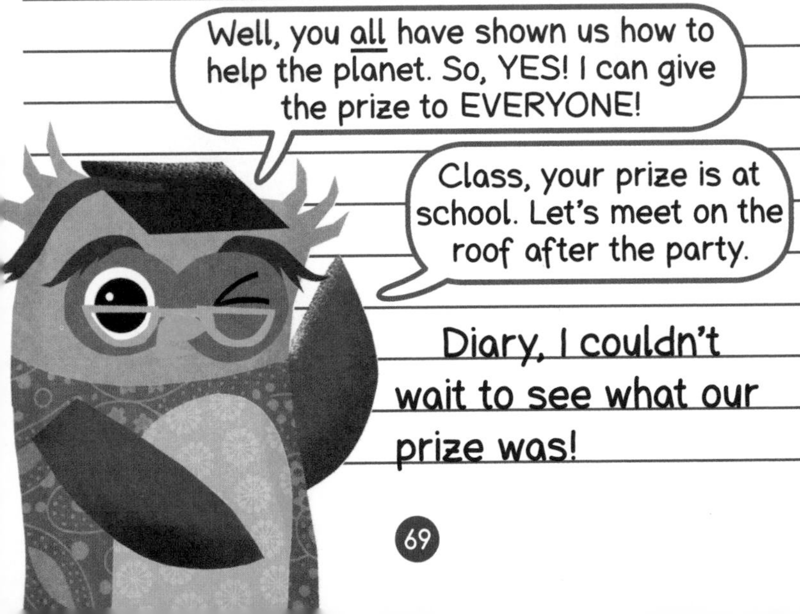
Well, you all have shown us how to help the planet. So, YES! I can give the prize to EVERYONE!
Class, your prize is at school. Let's meet on the roof after the party.

Diary, I couldn't wait to see what our prize was!

After the party, we flew over to school and found our prize . . .

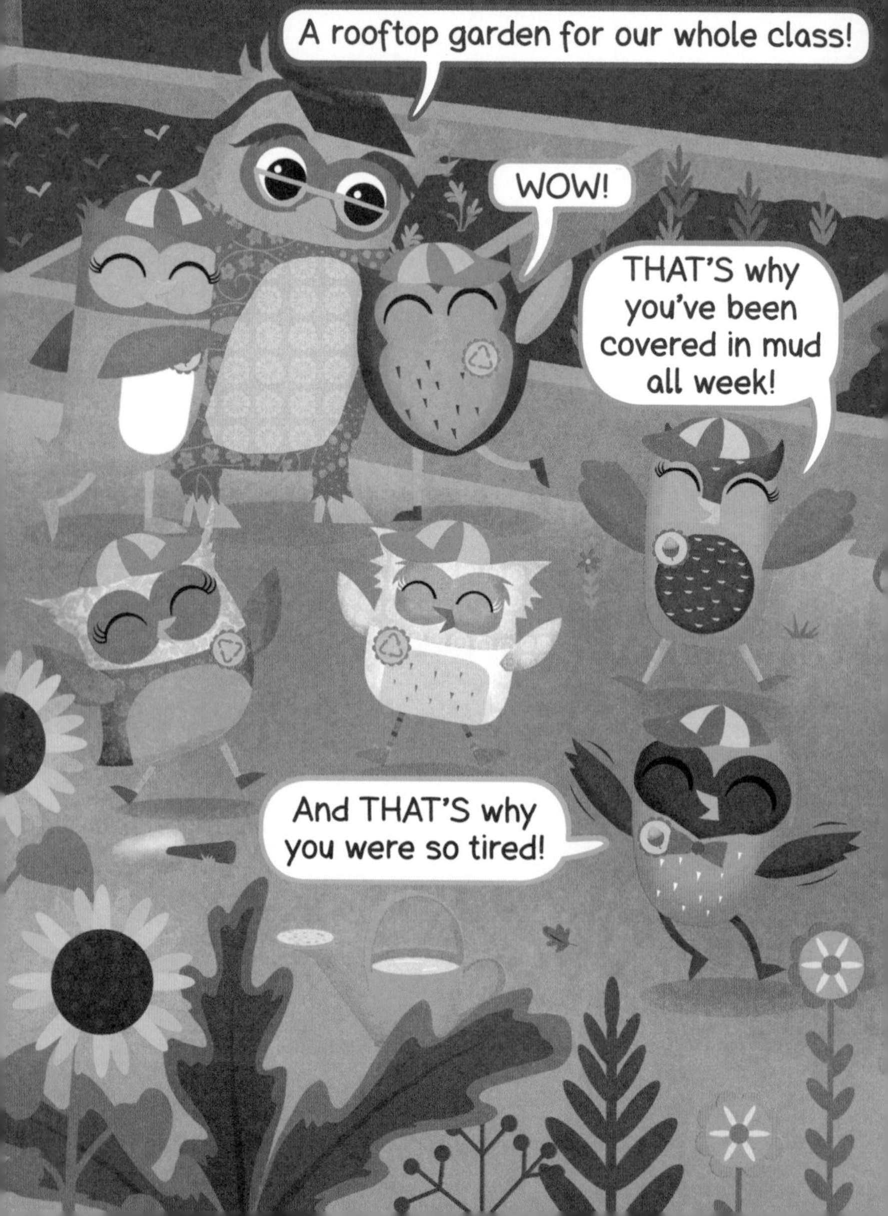
A rooftop garden for our whole class!
WOW!
THAT'S why you've been covered in mud all week!
And THAT'S why you were so tired!

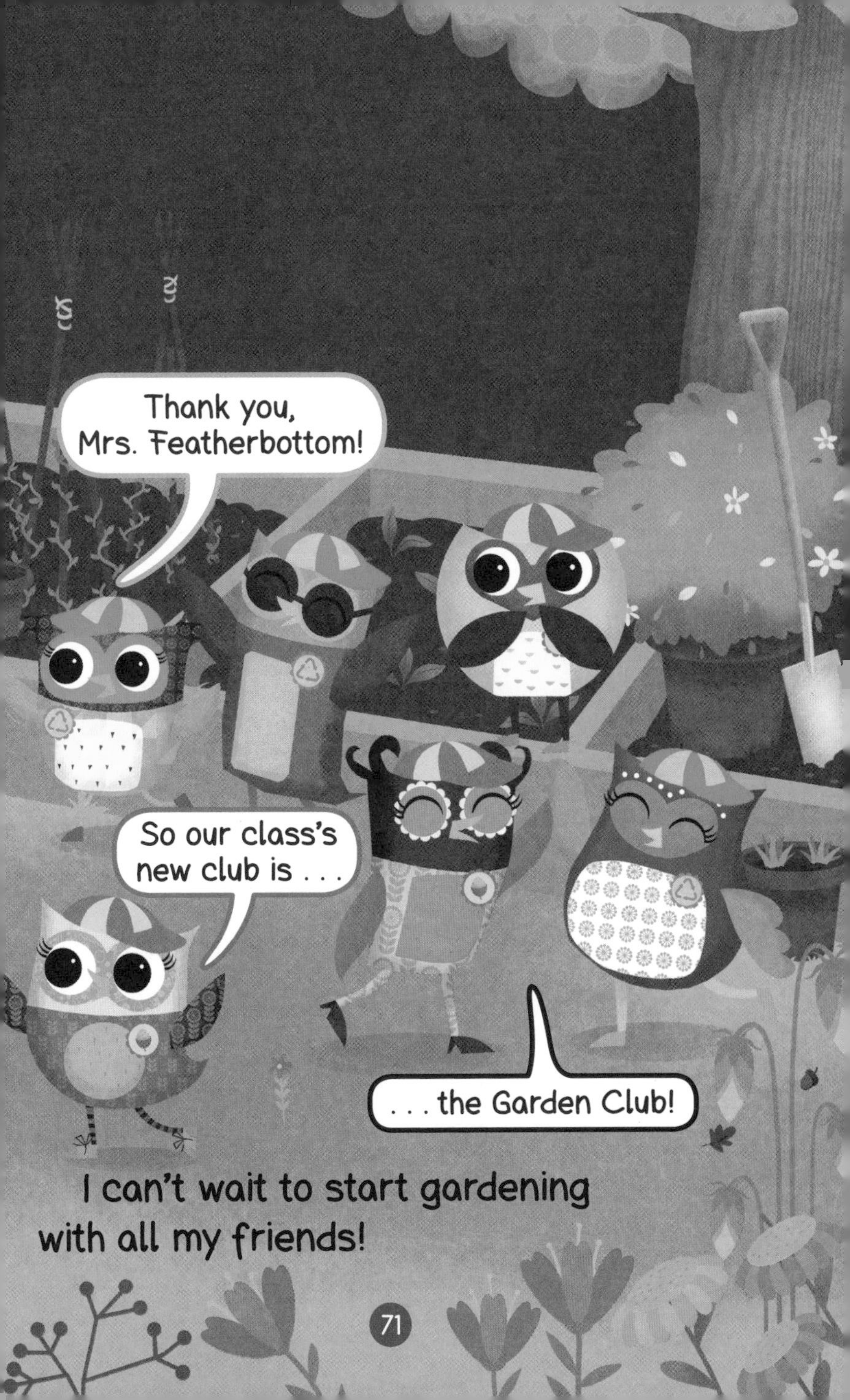
Thank you, Mrs. Featherbottom!
So our class's new club is . . .
. . . the Garden Club!

I can't wait to start gardening with all my friends!

Diary, I've had the BEST week! Turns out, looking after the world around you isn't just important – it's fun, too! (Especially when you work together!)

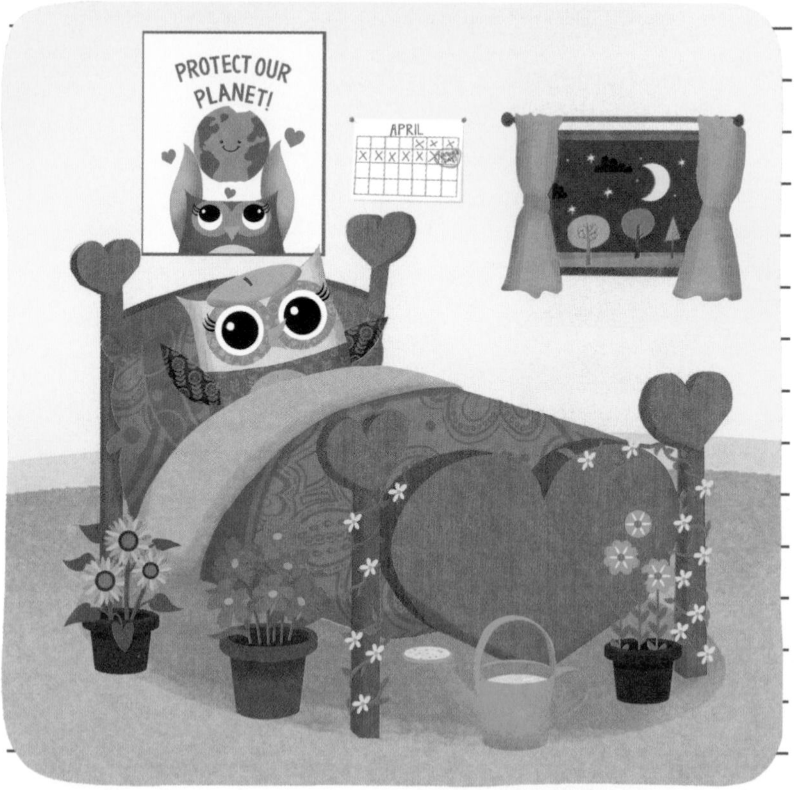
PROTECT OUR PLANET!
APRIL

I'm so lucky to live on this **FLAPTASTIC** planet with so many great friends. That's the real prize. See you next time!

Rebecca Elliott was a lot like Eva when

she was younger: She loved making things and
hanging out with her best friends. Now that
Rebecca is older, not much has changed —
except that her best friends now include her
two sons, Benjy and Toby. She still loves
making things, like stories, cakes, music, and
paintings. But as much as she and Eva have in
common, Rebecca cannot fly or turn her head
all the way around. No matter how hard she tries.

Rebecca is the author of several picture books,
the young adult novel PRETTY FUNNY FOR A
GIRL, and the bestselling UNICORN DIARIES and
OWL DIARIES early chapter book series.

OWL DIARIES

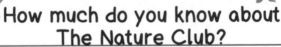

How much do you know about The Nature Club?

What is the Nature Club's goal? What activity helps them come up with it?

How does Eva feel about not being able to work with Lucy and Hailey? Have you ever felt this way?

Sue says she's feeling sad this week. Find two times when Sue seems to be acting out because of her mood.

Mrs. Featherbottom has been working hard all week to build the school garden. Who noticed that she was behaving strangely? What did they notice?

The Nature Club and the Recycle Club have different goals and take action in different ways. Which club would you join and why? Write and draw your answer.

scholastic.com/branches